AS THE FILM UNWOUND, NICK CARTER UNDERSTOOD WHY THE LATE-NIGHT BRIEFING HAD BEEN SO URGENT

The film clips showing Cuban refugees entering the United States revealed a withered old man in a wheelchair—Julio Romero, of Matanzas, Cuba.

But something about the frail figure did not seem quite right! Careful scrutiny exposed a cunning deception. Actually the man was broad-shouldered, barrel-chested, and the powerful muscles that moved in his legs belied the need of the wheelchair.

Nick Carter had the film clips run through three more times to make absolutely certain, and each viewing further confirmed the chilling truth —the man in the wheelchair was none other than Killmaster's most ruthless adversary: the incredibly evil mastermind of the Red Chinese spy network, the monster who went by the code name JUDAS.

Mr. Judas was back! Nick Carter had just watched him enter the United States!

D0273082

THE NICK CARTER/KILLMASTER SERIES

NICK CARTER

A Killmaster Spy Chiller

DANGER KEY

AWARD BOOKS
NEW YORK

Dedicated to

The Men of the Secret Services

of the

United States of America

Titles are also available at discounts in quantity lots for industrial or sales-promotional use. For details write to Special Projects Division, Award Books, 235 East 45th Street, New York, N.Y. 10017.

Copyright © MCMLXVI by
Universal Publishing and Distributing Corporation.
Produced by Lyle Kenyon Engel.
All rights reserved, including the right to
reproduce this book or portions thereof in any form.

"Nick Carter" is a registered trademark
of The Conde Nast Publications Inc.,
registered in the United States Patent Office.

AWARD BOOKS are published by:
Universal-Award House, Inc., a subsidiary of
Universal Publishing and Distributing Corporation,
235 East Forty-fifth Street, New York, N.Y. 10017

Manufactured in the United States of America

DANGER KEY

Chapter 1

She was not altogether naked.

A wispy triangle of white silk was tucked about her tanned, shapely midsection, while a matching fragment fought a losing battle to restrain twin mounds of full, sculptured loveliness.

Her ash-blonde hair streamed out behind in a way that made it seem almost part of the speeding white convertible.

The causeway along which she was hurtling was a fragile ribbon of concrete against the vast expanse of unrippled blue water. A quarter of a mile down its length stood the fisherman.

He smiled as he watched her approach—a wide, handsome smile that matched the girl, the car, the Florida keys in season. As she slowed, turning off onto the causeway's narrow shoulder, he waved cheerfully and reeled in his line, and the blonde waved back and blew him a kiss.

Love and leisure in a warm climate—what more could a man ask for?

The car suddenly surged forward, tires screaming against the tarmac. The fisherman's smile disintegrated. He stumbled backward, fell. The grillwork caught him full in the face, hurling him back against the guard rail. The blonde spun the wheel hard. With a grating roar of metal, the car sideswept the rail, peeling the man off it as if he were an extra coat of paint. His body vanished beneath the wheels. The blonde brought the car to a skidding stop. Glancing over her shoulder, she threw it into reverse and shot back over the crushed, broken remains, then forward again—and this time she didn't stop.

Captain Clegg's charter fishing boat had come hugging out from under the causeway in time for him to see the blonde in the white convertible roar away. The hit-and-run victim was still alive when he reached him.

"Mister, what happened?" he asked. "Can you hear me?"

The face was a bloody mask from which the features had been wiped as if by a rag. Eyelids fought their way open. Sightless eyes stared into his—puzzled, interrupted in important work. Mucus, spotted with blood, ran down what was left of a chin. The raw meat of the lips moved, the throat thickened as the muscles in it worked. "Pa . . ." The man took several chugging breaths. "Pa . . . okay . . ." he gasped.

Then the strength was gone. The eyes rolled back to their more important work. The remains of the face went slack.

Robyn's pale white limbs glimmered in the firelight. She was kneeling on the cushions of the couch, superbly naked, legs drawn up under her, the tinted nipples pointing, her lovely face flushed, her blue eyes bright with impatience. She put down her martini glass and said "Mmm" as Nick Carter entered, fresh from the shower. She tugged at the towel which he had modestly looped around his middle. It came away easily. "Double mmm," she murmured as she studied his readiness. Nick slid onto the couch beside her, his hand moving down over her taut little buttocks. He leaned forward, his lips brushing the back of her neck lightly.

The sharpness of the telephone's jangle made them both start.

"Oh, no!" she wailed. "He promised!"

"Robyn, other people *do* have my number," said Nick, as he reached past her and picked up the phone. He said only four words into the receiver. "What time?" and, after a pause, "All right." And Robyn knew from the set of his jaw and the way the steel-gray eyes had switched from hot to cold that it was *them*. AXE—America's supersecret counterintelligence agency.

"Two hours until plane time," he said to her now. "Will you bring the car back into Manhattan?"

"Oh no!" she repeated brokenly. "He promised that this time you'd have your full vacation."

Nick said, "He wouldn't send for me if it wasn't really important."

Robyn nodded through her tears. She knew that was so. They were in the same deadly business. And she was just as likely to be called suddenly to a new assignment. She sat bolt upright, wiped at her eyes with the back of one hand, and said, "It'll only take us an hour to get out there. Let's make the most of the time left."

Nick grinned. That was his Robyn. He thought back over the dozens of assignments and the dozens of lovely girls who had come between them over the years. Few of them could match her, for she alone understood that the telephone always had to be answered—that he was, in short, agent N3 of AXE, and that his life was not his own.

"Let's see," he mused, "where was I?" Robyn pointed to the back of her neck and, with a smile, he bent to kiss it, his hands moving up over her full, lovely breasts, feeling the nipples stiffen beneath his caresses.

It was after midnight when Nick Carter's plane landed at National Airport, and it took his cab more than an hour to reach downtown Washington through the snow-snarled streets. A raw March wind was blowing off the Potomac as he hurried into the Amalgamated Press and Wire Service Building on Dupont Circle. The night security man took him straight to the sixth floor. Not to Hawk's office, however, but to the projection room. All very strange, thought Nick, and with the smell of emergency about it.

Hawk's presence in the building at this ungodly hour suggested the same thing. The head of AXE was fanatical about keeping regular office hours. But here he sat, hunched forward in his seat in the smoky gloom, looking tense and impatient.

"Sorry about the delay, sir," said Nick. "Weather foul-up."

"Sit down, N3." Hawk pressed a button at the side of his seat and picked up a small hand mike. "You can go ahead," he told the projectionist. "Make sure the film clips are in the correct sequence."

A Boeing 707 appeared on the screen. It was taxiing to a stop. The airstair was rolled out to it, followed by a cluster of health and immigration officials.

"Eight hundred a week," said Hawk, speaking around the dead cigar in his thin-lipped mouth as the two men stared at the screen. "That's the rate at which the Cuban refugees have been airlifted in to this country over the past year. Aliens from a Communist country with which we have no diplomatic relations, no intelligence cooperation," he added, with a sidelong glance at his top operative. "A security nightmare. It's almost as if we had thrown the gates wide open and invited every power to send in their top people."

The Boeing's door was open now, the airstair in place, the health and immigration officials standing to either side of it. A stewardess propelled an empty, folded wheelchair onto the platform and the officials handed it along to the bottom of the stairs, where an attendant opened it. "Here's our man now," said Hawk, as three more stewardesses appeared in the 707's doorway. Between them they supported a feeble-looking old man wrapped in a heavy overcoat and scarf, his hat pulled down over his head. He was wearing mittens.

Hawk pressed the button. "Sound, please," he said to the projectionist.

". . . first off the plane is the oldest passenger, 72-year-old Julio Fernandez Romero of Matanzas, Cuba," announced a voice on the soundtrack. "He is sponsored by his son and daughter-in-law, Mr. and Mrs. Eduardo Romero of Fort Myers."

"This sequence was taken eleven months ago," said Hawk, "at Miami International Airport. The CIA photographs every arriving refugee. But, as with all the other elaborate screening procedures, it's simply inadequate to the task."

Nick shot him an inquiring glance. Hawk was chewing his cigar savagely. "Any Boy Scout of average intelligence, let alone a professional espionage agent, could waltz through all our precautions in five minutes flat. As a matter of fact, they have. AXE agents have come in from Cuba with the refugees and have passed through the Opa-Locka Detention Center undetected."

Nick's dark eyebrows rose in surprise. "And this Romero," he said, turning back to the screen and watching as the stewardesses helped the old man down the stairs. "Whose little boy is he?"

"We know one thing," replied Hawk. "He isn't Julio Romero of Matanzas. That Romero never left Cuba. His body was found buried in a shallow grave near Varadero Airport some three weeks after this man arrived in Miami. The Cubans immediately notified U.S. authorities, but by then it was too late, of course."

"He'd already been processed through Opa-Locka?"

Hawk nodded sourly. "His son and daughter-in-law had picked him up and started back to Fort Myers. Perhaps they saw through his disguise. At any rate, they didn't get very far. They were found murdered thirty miles outside Opa-Locka. On the highway that runs through the Everglades. The Tamiami Trail, is it?" He opened a folder on the seat beside him and handed Nick a paper. "Here's the official report."

Nick scanned it quickly. "The thirteen-year-old granddaughter, too," he said grimly.

"Very slick job," replied Hawk. "Weeks were wasted on the rape angle alone. And the savagery of the throat slittings—it all looked very spontaneous. An abandoned, blood-soaked car. The bodies dragged into the swamp. Signs of a struggle. The old man missing but for quite a while presumed kidnaped because of the manner in which he was dragged from his wheelchair along the ground to the other car. Very slick, indeed. The local police blundered about for weeks before the CIA uncovered the fact that the real Romero had never reached the U.S.—at which point they took over."

"And when did AXE enter the picture?"

A faintly pained look crossed Hawk's face. "Too late, I'm afraid, to do anything but pick up the pieces. Now here," he said abruptly, pointing to the screen. "This is interesting. Watch carefully." Nick did as "Julio Romero" was lowered into the wheelchair at the bottom of the airstair. Suddenly his hat was knocked askew by those helping him and his face became momentarily visible between their ministering forms. "Hold it there," said Hawk, speaking into the mike. "The closeup, please."

The projectionist made some adjustments, and the face—magnified a dozen times—flashed on the screen. The first thing Nick noticed was that it was curiously smooth and unlined for a man of his apparent age. Near the hairline were barely visible marks, possibly scars.

"If two of the three CIA agents working on the Romero case hadn't been killed in very suspicious hit-and-run accidents earlier this week," said Hawk, "chances are I wouldn't have had this sequence replayed. How serious *that* would have been, you'll see when we run it over in slow motion."

While the projectionist rewound the film, Hawk briefly summarized the CIA's ten-month investigation of the Romero case. Nelson Machado had covered the Cuban end; Juan Ochoa, Florida. Their control was Miami-based Ralph Benson. "Machado's reports," said Hawk, pointing to a thick manila folder on the seat beside him. "Required reading. Interpreted individually, they don't add up to much," he said, "but the cumulative effect is quite different. Harrowing is almost too mild a word. You'll see what I mean."

"Was Machado one of the hit-and-run victims?"

Hawk nodded. "The other was Ochoa," he said. "He was killed yesterday while fishing on a causeway in the Florida keys. He was on to something. What, we don't know—thanks to Benson," he added acidly.

Although Ochoa had acted with incredible stupidity, Hawk held his control responsible for the resulting mess. "Ochoa was not a professional," he said. "He was a Cuban refugee recruited by the CIA to keep them informed on developments in Miami refugee circles. He should never have been on a case like this. Or, if on it, he should have been kept on a tight leash. Instead, Benson allowed him to roam far afield and to report at infrequent intervals.

"On the morning he was killed," Hawk continued, staring fiercely at his dead cigar, "Ochoa called Miami control—on an open line, mind you—from Big Pine Key and told him that he was on his way to meet some woman he'd gotten involved with. He asked Benson to meet him that night at a certain cocktail lounge on Marathon Key, that he'd have the Romero case wrapped up by then and would give him all the details."

Nick couldn't suppress a grim smile at the mounting list of deadly errors. "Did Benson go?" he asked, not really believing it possible.

"He did," replied Hawk. "And not only that. When Ochoa didn't show, he drove on out to Big Pine and made inquiries about him." Nick shook his head in amazed disbelief. "Of course he didn't come right out and say where is so-and-so, the CIA agent," Hawk continued dryly. "He posed as a reporter from some magazine interested in interviewing the famous Peruvian sports fisherman, Pedro Villareal. That was the cover Ochoa had been using."

"Benson sounds like the prime candidate for a third hit-and-run accident."

Hawk shot him a funny look. "If that happens," he said, "you'll be the first to know about it." Nick stared at him. The head of America's super-secret intelligence agency was not smiling, however. His leathery features were deadly serious. He said: "The real Benson has been brought in from the cold, as they say. You'll take his place. He's your height, your general build. Editing will match your appearance with his and will provide you with the necessary personality dossier, plus recordings of his voice which you can study. You will then return to Big Pine Key and continue to bumble clumsily about. Our hope is that Ochoa's call to Benson was monitored, that Benson himself was observed on Big Pine. On the off chance he wasn't, though, you're to make every mistake in the book that will help reveal the fact you're a U.S. intelligence agent. But don't overact, of course. You're to draw the enemy out, not get yourself killed."

A voice squawked at Hawk's elbow. He picked up the mike and said, "Yes, run it now, please."

The overhead lights dimmed and once again the Boeing 707 came taxiing onto the screen—but in slow motion this time. The stewardesses moved with weird, dreamlike slowness as they helped the old man down the airstairs. "Now watch this," said Hawk, as the man's overcoat became briefly entangled in the handrail and came open.

Nick whistled softly. His trained eye had immediately

noted that the overcoat was not as heavy as it first appeared, but that the torso it shielded was! The man's age and frailty were largely deceptive. He was actually broad-shouldered, even barrel-chested, and when the film was run a third time, frame by frame, Nick could even make out the bunching muscles of the "old man's" powerful thighs as they worked to support him.

"The arms and hands are of particular interest," said Hawk. "Sequence 11-A, please," he said into the mike. It was the one immediately following the man's hat coming askew, and showed him adjusting it as a stewardess wheeled him along the tarmac to the arrival area. His arms and hands moved stiffly, as if they were crippled. Or mechanical.

"Now look at this closeup," said Hawk. It was an amazing magnification job. Clear and sharp. The hands were pulpy and unarticulated inside the mittens—like hand-shaped mudpacks, or inflated rubber gloves. A patch of skin showed between the left-hand mitten and the sleeve of the overcoat. It was shiny, unreal, with an unnatural texture.

Nick felt the hair on the back of his neck rise.

Now he understood the urgency of this late-night briefing. There was only one individual in the world who looked as if he had been put together with bits and pieces of inanimate objects. His machinations, and those of his masters, were the immediate concern of AXE. And the man who knew him best was Special Agent Carter, who had earned for himself the title of Killmaster.

Nick had the film clips run three more times to make absolutely certain. But each viewing only further confirmed the chilling truth—that the master spy and brutal killer for the Red Chinese, the man whose code name was Judas, *was here in the United States!*

Chapter 2

The battered red sports car wove erratically in and out of the stream of traffic traveling south on the Overseas Highway.

The man behind its wheel wore wrap-around smoked glasses and a gaudy aloha shirt. Charles Mackley, stringer for *Pic* Magazine, was handsome but graying, with a dissolute air about him. Strictly a wornout item—like the camera and typewriter on the seat beside him and his apartment in a run-down section of Miami.

He gave the car ahead a taste of his horn—a hideous glockenspiel-like racket. Behind his smoked glasses, he winced. For Mackley was not Mackley, nor was he Ralph Benson, the CIA agent to whom this disguise came so naturally. He was Nick Carter, and of all the personality changes that AXE's Editing Department had engineered for him over the years this one grated against his own nature the most.

Nick had met the real Benson through top-level CIA contacts in Miami and had come away from the meeting with a bad taste in his mouth. *A drunk!* The man was dangerous—to himself and to others. "It's like metal fatigue," was how Benson's superior had put it to Nick. "Been in it too long. Secret tippling for about six months now. Lucky to be getting out alive. We'll give him a clerical job in Communications until you've finished with his cover, then bounce him."

Benson was not the only nasty surprise wrapped up in this assignment. Hawk had sprung the other. "You'll carry none of your usual equipment," he had told N3. "Judas has dealt with us before. There must be nothing on your person which could alert him to the fact that AXE has replaced the CIA on this case."

Two chilling thoughts kept pulsing through Nick's mind, and he knew that they must be giving Hawk nightmares, too. The first was that Judas had already been in the U.S. for almost a year, operating with absolute impunity. The second grew out of Machado's reports from Cuba. Every other one had dealt with the disappearance of Red Chinese technicians. Peking's Embassy in Havana had complained that they were the victims of CIA infiltrators and demanded that security be tightened; the Cuban government had denied the allegations and charged, in turn, that the "technicians" were really espionage agents who were being funneled through Cuba to other parts of Latin America. Machado's own conclusion: they were actually Florida bound, using the refugees' small-boat exodus to the keys as their cover!

On arriving at Big Pine Key, Nick checked into the posh Sea-Top Hotel. It was where Ochoa had stayed while posing as the wealthy Peruvian sports fisherman. Overtipping somehow seemed Mackley-Benson's style, so Nick did, and the bellhop's sneer grew bolder. After he'd gone, Nick checked the room he'd been given for electronic bugs, then stripped down to his shorts and went out onto the sun-filled balcony.

Four stories beneath him, an elegant curve of cabañas swept down to the private beach and yacht basin. Within the curve was an Olympic-length swimming pool fringed on all sides by rows of mattressed steamer chairs on which the hotel's customers were already getting their $50-a-day tans. Nick took a deep breath of sea air, flexed his knees, and did a set of the yoga exercises that enabled him to squeeze out of tight corners and hold his breath for long, precious minutes. His body was the only weapon he was carrying on this assignment. He had an idea he'd be using it. Soon.

He took a shower, then got dressed and set out to find Eddie Clegg.

Nick had found the item in the local news sheet he had bought in the lobby on his way in. FISHERMAN KILLED ON CAUSEWAY ran the head. "Pedro Villareal, 38, Peruvian sports fisherman, was killed by a hit-

and-run driver on the causeway linking Big Pine with No Name Key last Wednesday. Eddie Clegg, captain of the charter fishing cruiser *Conchboy II,* was the first to reach his side. He reported that he must have been killed instantly. Sheriff Sam Grainger promises a thorough investigation of the mishap."

Nick found Captain Clegg at the end of a small weather-beaten wooden jetty that reached out on barnacled piles into Florida Bay. "You want to try for tarpon off Loggerhead Bank?" yelled the charter captain as he swung the cruiser out, spinning the wheel and looking astern to watch the clearance past the piling. "They're in the shallow flats there this time of year."

"No, I want to go to Peligro Key," said Nick.

Clegg glanced sharply at him. Beneath the tattered baseball cap his scrawny face was thin and bloodless, the color of tobacco dust. "No fish there," he said, a toothpick sliding from one side of his mouth to the other. "All that underwater construction scared 'em away."

"I'm not after fish," said Nick. "I want pictures of Aquacity. That's what I'm down here for. Assignment from *Pic.*"

That was the cover story, at any rate, that Editing had cooked up for him. The underwater "Disneyland" being built by Texas oil millionaire A. K. Atchinson had generated a lot of excitement when a scale model had been put on display at the New York World's Fair. Photographers and reporters had been banned, however, from the actual construction site, now more than a year old. Atchinson was a crusty old eccentric who placed privacy before publicity.

Clegg shook his head. "Nossir, I'm not riskin' my boat," he said. "Couple of Seminoles got shot at the other day when they tried to land there to hunt turtles." Nick's dark eyebrows rose in surprise. "I'm not kiddin'," insisted Clegg. "Old A. K.'s bodyguards won't let nobody even get near the key."

"What about the construction men?" asked Nick. "I read he had at least a hundred fifty highly trained divers working on the site."

"They live out there," said Clegg. "In his house, maybe. It's big enough. They never come in. I got a buddy who delivers the groceries out there," he snickered. "He told me about all the dirty statues A. K.'s got around. He's a real horny old guy, I hear. My buddy says he never sees no construction guys. He thinks all that food is fer A. K.'s harem." He exploded into a wheezing, gap-toothed laugh.

Nick made a mental note to follow up on Peligro on his own. To Clegg he said, "Make it Loggerhead, then."

They were out of the harbor now. Clegg gunned the motor and they picked up speed. Ahead, a long causeway ran along the horizon, joining Big Pine with a smaller key dotted with neat white houses, mangroves and scrubby pines. "That's No Name," said Clegg, in reply to Nick's question about it. "No kiddin'. That's what they call it. Them houses there along the water—that's Senior City. Atchinson built it a couple of years back. What they call a pilot project—for old folks."

Nick pointed to the causeway. "That's where that South American fellow was killed the other day, isn't it?" he asked. Clegg's grin vanished. He got very busy with the job of steering. "I saw in the paper that you witnessed it," Nick continued, watching the charter captain carefully from the corner of his eye. The effect was electric. Clegg's hands tightened on the wheel. He swallowed heavily.

"How come you're so interested in that?" he muttered.

"How come you're so jumpy about it?"

"I didn't see nothin'. I was under the causeway when it happened." They rode on in silence for a moment, then Clegg said, "Here, take the wheel a minute. I got to check the motors. See the course? Two twenty-five." He straightened up from the stool and headed aft. Nick took his place. He had a pretty good idea of what was coming next. One thing about Clegg: He was obvious, you could hear him thinking a mile away. Nick waited until the other man had had time enough to reach the fire extinguisher and unsheath the utility knife which hung next to it, then counted to three—the number of paces he knew it would take the captain to return to his side.

Nick's arm swung even as his body turned. It sliced through the air in a swift and deadly arc that exploded against Clegg's neck. The man gasped and staggered back. Nick cut the motor and rose from the control stool in one easy, fluid motion. His leg shot out in a swift upward kick, while the hard edge of his right hand slammed into the cartilage of Clegg's nose. The knife clattered to the deck.

Nick picked it up, tested its sharpness against his thumb, then pressed its point into Clegg's knotted neck. "Agh!" The sound forced itself out of the man's throat. His shoulders jumped spasmodically. "Stop!" he gasped. "Take the knife away an' I'll tell you everythin' I know. . . ."

Nick kept the knife there, and Clegg told him anyway— all about the blonde in the white convertible, and "Villa- real's" last words before he died. *Pa, okay,* mused Nick. Could mean anything. A Spanish word. Maybe even Seminole, as Clegg seemed to think. Their words all ended in *okays.* The knife jabbed deeper. "The girl," urged Nick.

"Name's Ingra something," gasped Clegg. "Her pa's a professor. Retired. Lives in Senior City. She comes here to see him." The knife bit again, a neat half circle in the flesh, and paused. "Bastard!" Clegg snarled. "You don't need to stick me with no knife. Anybody around here could have told you the same thing—that she ran him down on purpose. She was having a big loud affair with him. They had a lovers' spat that same morning. Lots of people saw it—out on the beach. She stormed off. An hour later—splat! Investigation? Ha! The sheriff an' her are like that." Fingers together, leering.

Maybe Clegg had more to tell, but Nick knew that getting it out of him would mean playing rougher. He decided against it. His job this time was only to find and fix the enemy, not fight him. "All right," he said, resheathing the knife. "Back to Big Pine."

Ashore, Nick doubled back on his tracks—just in time to see Clegg hurrying away from the jetty. He waited until the charter captain had a good lead on him, then followed. The trail ended in front of a vast fat man who sat on a folding chair outside the local 5 & 10, having his shoes shined. The obscene mountain of jelly wore a holster and a star. Sheriff Grainger in the flesh, thought Nick, The conversation between the two men was brief but intense. It ended with the sheriff's rising and lumbering with ponderous haste toward his car. Clegg watched him drive off, then turned and started back in Nick's direction.

"May I help you?" chirped the bright-eyed old lady behind the counter as she put down her knitting. Nick glanced around, saw that it was the "Lower Keys Tourist Bureau" into which he had dodged, and murmured vaguely, "Brochures." From the corner of his eye he watched Clegg's reflection pass by the window. "Yes, as a matter of fact, you could," he said now, turning to her. "Have you anything on Peligro Key?"

"Oh no, that's private property," she said rather sharply. "We have this, though, on Aquacity." She handed Nick a brochure.

"It's Peligro itself that interests me," said Nick. He made a wild stab in the dark. "I understand it has a colorful history."

"Oh, *that!*" Her eyes glistened enthusiastically behind her rimless glasses and she handed him another brochure.

Halfway through the door a sudden thought struck Nick. "Oh, by the way," he said, turning back to her, "do you know of any Seminole word that has a sound like 'pa, okay'?"

Her eyes seemed unnaturally bright. "It's pronounced Pa-*hay*-okee," she chirped shrilly. "It means River of Grass—the old Seminole name for the Everglades, you know."

He thanked her and left. Outside, a warning signal ticked in his brain. Nick stopped, quickly doubled back to the window and glanced in. She was at the telephone, dialing furiously.

He turned away. Maybe it didn't mean anything. Just a coincidence. But N3 didn't believe in coincidences. He slowed down. He dawdled, looking in windows. When he thought he'd allowed her enough time, he glanced over his shoulder. His eyes leapt at an image, caught it, and held it even as his swift gaze flickered away. The street was fairly crowded and the man wasn't even looking at him, but Nick knew he was being followed.

Chapter 3

It was called The Fish Net, and Nick had never in his life been inside it, but the minute the bartender saw him he grinned and poured a water tumbler full of gin. "Just bitters, right?" he said, sliding the Angostura bottle along the bar toward him.

Nick nodded numbly as he absorbed the neon-lit fish net decor, the mounted swordfish, photos of men holding trophies. A florid-faced type on the stool next to him turned. "How you doin'?" he said, his voice thick and indistinct with liquor. "You ever find that South American guy you were lookin' for?"

Nick mentally placed Benson on a spit in hell and gave it a good half turn. He nodded, glancing past the drunk, watching the open door. The man who'd been tailing him along Big Pine's main drag paused outside, not looking in but absorbing it all from the corner of his eye. A match flared in his cupped hands as he lit a cigarette. He was wearing skin-tight dungarees tucked into cowboy boots. A Stetson was pulled low on his face, but the match illuminated the hatchetlike features clearly. The high cheekbones, burnished skin—ask a Seminole question, thought Nick grimly, you get a Seminole tailing you. It figured, about as clearly as everything else in this crazy, mixed-up mess.

"You staying at the Sea-Top?" the florid-faced drunk persisted. Nick nodded. Drunk said: "Not me, not this time." Nick glanced past him again. The Seminole had vanished. "You phone downstairs for a deck of cards in that tip-hungry dump," the drunk was saying, "and the bellhop delivers them in fifty-two separate trips—one lousy card at a time!" Nick picked up his drink and moved down the bar. He couldn't stand comic drunks. He settled on the stool nearest the window and took out the brochure on Peligro.

Peligro Key derives its name, he read, *from the Spanish word for danger, and was so named because it represented a navigational hazard to the Spanish treasure fleets bound from Florida's west coast to. . . .*

The roar of a supercharged engine brought Nick's head up fast. A blonde in a white two-seater had just executed a skillful racing shift through third into second as she swerved out of a side street. Now she brought the low-slung powerhouse to a screeching halt outside The Fish Net.

"Wow!" It came from the bartender, standing behind Nick.

"You mean her, the car, or Boris Karloff there?" muttered the drunk, who had come forward at the noise.

"I mean I can't figure out why she's coming in here," said the bartender. "The Sea-Top's more her style."

Not bothering to open the low door, the blonde now swung one brown leg and then the other over the side, showing her thighs under the short black dress almost to her waist as she slipped to the pavement. "Wow!" It was Nick who said it this time, and he didn't mean the car.

"Boris Karloff comes in occasionally," persisted the bartender, "but not her."

The man they called Karloff actually looked more like a young Peter Lorre. His face was soft, pretty, unnaturally white, and, to make things worse, he was as bald as a rock. The overall effect was of a department store mannikin without its wig.

"Hello, Ingra!" sang the drunk in tune with "Hello, Dolly." "You slumming tonight?"

Ingra! N3's mind snapped to attention.

"Hello, yourself." She smiled and turned toward Nick. It was the briefest of glances she gave him, but Nick's trained eye caught its full intensity. In that split second she had studied him as though she intended to memorize his face and file it away forever. Nick had done the same with her—but less in cold appraisal than in honest awe. Her hair was the palest ash blonde and shone almost silver under the bar's soft neon. He practically fell into the deep blue-green wells of her eyes. He saw the slow curve of a self-satisfied smile on her sensuous lips as she turned away, saying to the drunk, "Just a brief stop-off for me. Karl wants to talk fishing. I want to dance. We've compromised. I'll have one drink here and go on."

She moved past him, following the bald man to a table in the rear. So the drunk knew her? Nick was suddenly interested in him. "Extremely attractive girl," he said conversationally. "Known her long?"

"Met her a couple of times at the Sea-Top," the drunk said expansively. Nick asked how he'd feel about introducing him. "My pleasure," said the drunk, rising from his stool with excessive dignity and weaving toward the back. A number of obvious fisherman types had joined their table, and Nick saw the girl glance up hopefully as he approached. The drunk hammed it up with "my very old friend" before he realized he didn't know Nick's name. Everyone laughed in a friendly way and Nick introduced himself as Charles Mackley.

The bald man rose and said, "Orff. Karl Orff. That's two words, not as in Boris," and everyone laughed again.

Then Orff introduced Ingra Brand and the two sports fishermen. Eying Nick's camera, he said: "So. What brings you back to Big Pine a second time?"

Nick's heart wasn't the kind that skipped beats, but had it been, now was the time for it to skip a couple. Had that idiot Benson met Orff and forgotten to tell him? he wondered tensely. But he said casually, "My magazine wants to do a feature on Aquacity."

Orff watched him from beneath heavily lidded eyes. "And your piece on Pedro Villareal," he murmured in a high nasal whine that grated against Nick's nerves. "Is it completed?"

"The man's dead," said Nick, "so the article is also."

Ingra Brand rose abruptly, turned and walked over to the jukebox. Nick watched her. So did Orff. Smoke from the gold-tipped cigarette which drooped at the corner of his mouth went curling around his bald dome. "Villareal was her fiancée," he said—so softly that Nick had to lean forward to catch the words. As he did, he felt a soft, moist hand suddenly close around his. He glanced down. Orff was smiling up at him. "Don't feel badly at not remembering me," he purred. "You were—how should I put it—in your cups the other night."

Nick felt dangerously close to nausea. He took a long, hard slug of the gin and bitters he was still holding. But there was worse to come. Ingra glanced up from the juke-box as he approached and, smiling, said: "N-3." He managed not to react, but it was hard. Then he saw that she was pointing at the list of records. "I don't have any change," she said. "Number N-3, please. "The Girl from Ipanema." It's my favorite."

Coincidence? It had to be. What else?

He dropped a quarter in and she began to move her shoulders back and forth to the music, her eyes closed. Her black dress was low cut, tight under the strain of her full breasts, and they swayed gently with the move-ment. Some widow's weeds! thought Nick, eying her appreciatively. She smiled and moved toward him. "Care to trip the light et cetera?" she murmured. Her touch upon his arms was light but electric, her body move-ments subtle, rhythmic. The cool, voluptuous music of the Bossa Nova enveloped them and swept them away. Ingra sang the words softly against his chest, substitut-ing "Senior City" for "Ipanema."

Nick grinned. "So you're the girl from Senior City," he said, and there was a faintly hard edge to his voice. If she noticed it, she chose to ignore it. And Nick didn't pursue it either, but gave himself up temporarily to the pleasure of his senses. So perfectly matched were their two bodies and movements that neither was conscious of the mechanics of dancing. Her legs moved with his, and whatever she was feeling or thinking came out not in words, but translated itself instead into harmonious, al-most liquid motion.

The record ended. "You're awfully good," she said, "but sort of wasted in this place."

"I've been waiting to be discovered."

She gave a little laugh and drew away—but very slightly. "I think that can be arranged," she murmured, glancing toward Orff, who was deep in conversation with the two sports fishermen and the drunk.

Charles Mackley's graying, liquor-blurred features followed her gaze disinterestedly, but beneath Editing's disguise, N3's mind, eyes and subconscious were busy letting the "essence" of the bar's back room and its macabre occupants soak into him. What he got was a thousand jangling alarm bells. The conversation: too intense. Fishermen leaned back, told tall stories, laughed, drank it up. And then there was the drunk himself— suddenly no longer drunk. Also intense, listening, almost as if receiving instructions.

"We're going on to the Sea-Top, Karl," Ingra called out. "I don't suppose you'd care to join us?" Orff smiled and shook his head. "He's impossible when he gets started on fishing," she laughed, linking her arm in Nick's. They didn't take her white sports car, but walked the short distance to the hotel instead. "A beautiful moon-lit night," sighed Ingra at Nick's side. "With the trade winds blowing. I love the keys."

Mackley murmured assent while N3's mind thought of the two days he'd spent in Benson's Miami apartment, setting up the radio AXEmen call Oscar Johnson and getting the feel of the man. He remembered the filth, the bottles, the half-filled cans of beer everywhere. Nick put himself in the other man's shoes. He had come to the keys knowing Machado had been killed by a hit-and-run driver. Then Ochoa hadn't shown. Benson had started asking around. A bar would be a natural place. Totally unnerved by the news of Ochoa's death, he'd begun to drink hard, perhaps had even shot his mouth off. Then, like all hard drinkers, he'd remembered little or nothing of it the next day.

Nick stoked the fires under Benson's spit and gave it another half turn. This whole goddamned setup was beginning to get on his nerves. Nothing had gone right so far and he had an uneasy sensation that things would get worse before they got better. Nick Carter had been on jobs like this before and he knew the feeling.

The main street faded out in a stretch of sand and pulverized shells, and they went on through the parking lot into the Sea-Top's Bamboo Room. They ordered vodka martinis. A Cuban quintet was just getting up on the stand. "Shall we?" said Nick, as the quintet started on a bongo-rhythm arrangement of "The Way You Look To-night."

She still hadn't answered his question, but the hell with it for now, thought Nick. Ingra Brand was one of the most beautiful bundles of curves he'd ever held in his arms and she danced as though she were leading him straight to bed. As a matter of fact, maybe that was where the questions could best be answered, he mused as the dance moved them apart and drew them together, made them feel each other's warmth and the pulsa-tions that flowed from one to the other. Nick felt his pulse quicken as a moment of music brought her thighs against his. A warning buzzer rang in his brain. Watch yourself, N3 told himself, and willed his blood to cool.

The beat changed. Ingra smiled up at him. "The way you dance," she murmured, her voice a sigh of something very like fulfillment, her eyes luminous blue pools which had suddenly grown even deeper. "It's an experience . . . I've not had for quite some time. . . ." Her smile said the rest—not obviously, yet nonetheless unmistakably. "You know, of course, about my fiancée." She shuddered slightly. "I've felt his loss more strongly every day. . . ." She interrupted herself. "I shouldn't be talking to you like this."

They were dancing again, her hips swiveling against his with a motion that was less suggestion than demand. "One should say what one means, even at the risk of being misunderstood," murmured Nick, letting his hand wander in a suggestive little caress. Calculatingly, he gazed into her eyes, then lightly brushed his lips against the rich blonde mass of hair. Her eyes were on him again, watching his face, smiling at him, holding his eyes with the steadiness of her own. She was acting as if Ochoa-Villareal had been dead years rather than days, thought Nick. Either she was insatiable, or a consummate ac-tress. Or both.

"There's a beach I know. No one ever goes there." She was whispering, her lips parted and moist. "Just this side of the No Name Causeway." Her eyes roamed over his face and down his body as she gave him detailed instructions on how to reach it. Her breasts seemed to swell under his gaze.

No Name Causeway, thought Nick. Where Ochoa was killed—*by her,* according to Clegg. And Nick was to go on alone in his own car, she was saying now, and he was to wait for her there. She would go back to The Fish Net and tell Orff that she had a headache and was going home. And then she would drive out there and they would be together.

Nick studied her face, wondering if this was how she had lured Ochoa to his death. "Sounds delightful," murmured Charles Mackley, while Nick Carter uneasily recalled the right fender of her car. He'd gotten a good look at it as they had left The Fish Net earlier.

It was one of the most careless, blatantly obvious fender straightening jobs he'd ever seen.

Chapter 4

The tall anvil-shouldered man who had been standing in the shadows stirred at last. He glanced at the radium dial of his wrist watch. He had been motionless for nearly half an hour. Waiting. Not on the causeway itself, but just this side of it, in a grove of scrubby pines. His battered red sports car was parked a hundred yards down the highway, also screened by pines.

Despite the precautions, Nick couldn't rid himself of a feeling that he was being watched.

He'd first felt it on his way through the parking lot after Ingra had left him to return to The Fish Net. His sixth sense had warned him of a watcher, or at least of someone near him in the dark. He'd stepped out of the pool of light cast by the Bamboo Room's marquee and held to the shadows, taking a long, slow look around. But either his instinct had deceived him or someone was going to a lot of trouble to hide himself. After a few moments of watchful waiting he'd glided silently through the lot toward his car.

Habit had made him study its surfaces in search of new fingerprints, its locks for signs of tampering. Nothing. Then he'd circled it cautiously and had peered under the hood before getting in and driving off. Still nothing. And he had stopped along the highway a couple of times and doused his lights. But no car was following him.

So why couldn't he shrug off the feeling?

The distant roar of a racing supercharger warned him of her approach. Nick stepped cautiously out from between the trees and watched the white, low-slung two-seater approach. He waved. She waved back and turned off onto the shoulder of the highway. Even as he smiled, Nick's muscles tensed, ready to leap aside at the last moment if he had to. But she skidded to a stop a few yards short of him and slid demurely from the front seat, returning his smile.

Wordlessly they walked down to the edge of the water. The coral dust, left damp-packed by the going tide, made faint whining noises beneath their feet. She laughed at the sound and suddenly became alive with gaiety, insisting that they plunge into the breakers that curled softly beneath the new moon.

She kicked off her sandals and fumbled at the side zipper on her skirt. It began to part. She released it and it slid down her hips and fell to the sand. She stepped out of it, clad only in her bra and black bikini panties. Tossing her heavy blonde hair, she struck a stripper's pose, one hand across her breasts and the other over the rounded V of her crotch in a fig-leaf effect. Her eyes laughed up at him.

With almost childish delight, she continued the charade, swaying in time to nonexistent music as her hands went around in back and worked at the brassiere snap. It came free. Nick's blood raced as the gorgeous breasts sprang free.

She leaned over. Then, with a swift bending of her supple body, she came upright again, utterly nude. The bare flesh, white and gleaming against the darker patches of her tan, was a stunning revelation. The astonishingly full, ripe breasts stood out firmly, a delightful counterpoint to the flat plane of her stomach with the shadowy indented navel, the flare of her hips, the graceful tapering of her legs.

"And you?" she laughed. "Am I never going to see that obviously splendid body of yours?"

Behind Nick's grin was puzzlement at her rapid-change personality. He couldn't make her out. She was splashing in the waves like a little girl now, peeking playfully at him as he undressed. At other times, though, she seemed a fully mature woman. And what about that painted-over fender? Wasn't she also a cold-blooded killer?

As he waded toward her, she reached out a slender hand and clasped his wrist, her eyes moving admiringly along his broad shoulders and down the sinewy, tapering body. The child had disappeared from her face. She was a woman now, wanting, demanding.

His wet arms went around her. His lips crushed down on hers. Her marvelous breasts thrust against his chest and he could feel her body quivering. Their lips and tongues grew increasingly warm and searching. The kiss blazed and lingered; blazed again; and finally she drew back with a tiny choking sigh, her eyes swimming.

"God how I've wanted that," she breathed huskily.

He led her out of the water and up the dark beach to a natural rock shelter he'd noticed while undressing. She sank to the sand and he dropped to one knee beside her. The new moon had broken through the shifting clouds and he gazed deeply into her eyes, green now in its light. "You realize I don't know even the first thing about you?" he murmured, his hand tracing the soft lines of her neck and chin, then sliding down to feel the contours of one full, pointed breast. She began to tremble, her mouth forming the word "later." She seized his hand and slid it lower until it was stroking the silky softness at the very quick of her being.

He heard a car in the distance, and froze. It passed without stopping and a moment later he saw its red tail-lights moving along the causeway.

She pulled his head down and kissed him hungrily, expertly. Her fingers wandered over his body. Her half-closed eyes gleamed in the moonlight, her breath came quickly. Despite himself, he felt his own pulse quicken. A warning voice told him coldy that this woman was possibly an agent, almost certainly a killer. *Watch yourself, don't let go,* he told the unthinking blur that was the front part of his brain. *She's good, but not that good,* he repeated savagely. But it wasn't true. She was superb.

Nick felt her legs part beneath him, felt the bone-tight tautness of his own body sliding into her softness. Her hands caressed and fondled him with growing urgency, until at last her fingernails bit into his back and her mouth melted against his in supplication and hot desire. Their bodies tensed and arched and flowed together, thighs straining deliciously and mouths blending. Nick let himself go—all of himself but that one segment that was always an agent, on the alert for the dangerous, the unexpected.

She seemed to sense that part, and her lips began to search for it as if it were a physical thing, trailing provocatively over his ears . . . his eyes . . . his mouth . . . his throat. Her hands closed over the plunging muscles and felt the firmness of them. "Ohhh!" she moaned. "Closer, closer . . ."

His pulse began to race to catch up with hers, his whole being tingled with growing desire. He felt himself going, slipping over the edge . . . His senses dimmed. Her body shook and twisted with its need. Her legs scissored around him and her muscles strained to draw from him all the strength that he could give. It seemed to him that he was drowning beneath her onrushing desire, and yet that somehow she still eluded him, still held one part of herself in reserve, aloof from the turbulence of . . . what? . . . a battle . . . that's what this had become . . . a savage, ecstatic battle. . . .

He rolled her over and pulled her with him, fiercely jackknifing his desire home. And this time he found her! Each movement was a stab of ecstasy. She gasped suddenly, tore at his lips with her teeth. Her fingers clawed his chest. He swore softly and pulled her arms away, pinning them at her sides without losing his stride. Her movements quickened convulsively in time with his, and then in one last crazed moment they both forgot the hard sand beneath them, the distant surf, their separate identities—all but the exquisite bursting inside them as their whole beings seemed suddenly ignited, then liberated and free, floating away from the world on wave after shuddering wave of ecstasy . . .

The moment lingered and died.

They lay beside each other for a while, not touching. At last she shivered, hugging herself in a way that squeezed her breasts into two lovely globes of pearly flesh. The pink of the circlets seemed to darken as a rush of blood swelled the soft masses. Nick kissed her lightly on the tip of each, rose and walked over to where they had dropped their clothes. He picked them up and returned to her side, feeling unusually tired for a man to whom sex was as necessary as the very air he breathed.

He lay back on one elbow and watched her. Who was this woman? Which of the half-dozen erotic types which he had just explored was really her? The demure one, waiting to be aroused? The woman of the world, drawing him on and then holding him back? The siren, offering him a glimpse of what might be if he only followed her? The voluptuous concubine, leading him into strange paths and arousing him anew at every sensuous turn?

A car's motor broke the stillness. *Or any of them?* he wondered suddenly, alert, listening. The car passed in the distance without stopping. It nevertheless reminded him of a painted-over fender. Reminded him also that he was an agent, on assignment, and that time was rapidly running through his fingers.

He drew her down to lie quietly in his arms. "Ingra, sweetheart, tell me about yourself," he said, speaking with studied casualness as his lips trailed along the edge of her cheek.

She laughed. "There's not much to tell. Mine's been a dull life—except for tonight," she added, returning his kiss with sudden feeling.

"Everyone's life seems dull to them at times."

"Only seems?" she laughed, stressing the last word. "You've obviously never been employed on a government project!"

"And you have? What kind?"

"Well, that's classified, of course. But I'm in electronics. One of those boring top-secret projects. The kind where they lock you away for months at a time. I go quietly crazy and start climbing the walls, and then they send me down here to visit my father until I'm ready to submerge again for another six months." She ran her finger thoughtfully along the smooth, rippling muscles of his upper arm—over the skin graft Editing had used to cover the axe-shaped tattoo Nick wore above the right elbow. But she seemed not to notice the slight variation in texture, for she now gave the arm a quick, affectionate squeeze and said in a shaky voice: "God knows how I'm going to be able to stand it again after this."

He kissed her eyelids gently. "It isn't a line of work I'd exactly associate you with," he chuckled. "How did you happen to get into it?"

"My father." She sighed. "He was always working on some government project or other. My whole childhood was spent in synthetic, fenced-in scientific communities. Places like Los Alamos, Oak Ridge . . ."

Something clicked in Nick's mind. "Brand," he said. "Of course. Professor Gunther Brand."

"The one and only." She smiled. "You've heard of him?"

"Who hasn't? After all, he developed the atomic submarine."

"Yes, but that was all so long ago. He's retired now. Lives over there." She pointed along the causeway. "In Senior City."

Nick nodded. A gust of wind plucked at Ingra's discarded dress, scattered it with sand, and dropped it. The scrubby pines sighed and rustled. He turned his head.

"I love the keys," she sighed. "The lovely night trade winds. . . ."

"It's getting chilly. We ought to start back." Suddenly he swung toward her. "And what about Orff?" he asked. "Where does he fit into your life? A new romantic interest?"

She threw back her head and laughed. "God no, not poor Karl. He's just my father's doctor. Dad suffered a stroke a few months ago, you see, and. . . ."

She never finished the sentence. Nick was already in motion, whiplashing his body to one side. The sixth sense that had forewarned him of trouble so many times before had just sent up a sudden flare in his consciousness without giving him any reason why. Just in time, too. Steel-tipped cowboy boots plunged into the sand where he'd been lying. In one violent corkscrew of motion, Nick's body twisted up and struck a sledge-hammer blow against the unguarded face, catching the man off balance.

The girl screamed and leaped aside. Nick's bunched hands flashed. One low, in a feint, the other against the bronzed hatchet face that swayed above him. The Seminole staggered back and sideways against the rock outcropping. His hand reached inside his faded denim jacket, while his foot shot out. The steel tip of his boot hissed past Nick's face.

Nick crouched low, his muscles coiled like a snake's.

He caught the outstretched leg with both hands and yanked upward with all his strength. The Seminole's head slammed against the rocks and his upper body slid down its rough surface. Nick's arms flicked out, closing around the hand the Seminole still had inside his jacket. He twisted mercilessly. Something snapped in the Seminole's wrist. A high-pitched yelp of pain tore from his lips. Nick ripped open his jacket and slid the gun from its shoulder holster. As he did, he saw the star pinned to the man's shirt. The word DEPUTY SHERIFF was embossed on it.

Beautiful, thought Nick savagely. The perfect end to a perfect assignment. "Head for the car!" he yelled over his shoulder. One of AXE's cardinal rules stated firmly: *Never* get involved with the police unless you have pre-arranged an impenetrable cover that includes cooperation with them. Nick looked at the man writhing on the sand and decided things couldn't be worse.

The girl didn't reply. He swung around—to find his escape blocked by 350 pounds of charging flesh. Sheriff Grainger! Nick drew his right fist back. One fairly hard punch in the belly should do it. It would wind the sheriff but not hurt him, and give Nick a chance to reach the car.

To Nick's surprise, the sheriff halted abruptly and went into a crouch, his feet springing apart with amazing speed. His right arm cut across, his body swiveling with it. It was a classic *sumo* Parry Defense Against Underhand Thrust. Forearms met midway between the two bodies. What had appeared to be soft fat was as hard as steel, and the force of the sheriff's blow spun Nick's arm off-target and opened his guard for a crashing short-arm chin jab. The sheriff delivered it with a savage grunt—not of effort, but of triumph. There was something almost ritualistic about it, like the grunts and foot-stamping of a *yokozuma,* or grand champion, of *sumo* wrestling.

Even though momentarily incapacitated by surprise, Nick could have stopped the blow. The necessary counter-blow would, however, have killed the sheriff. Instead, Nick dodged backward, trying to move with the jab. The sheriff's stiff, locked wrist had not traveled far, perhaps two feet, but the heel of his palm, with fingers spread for rigidity, came up and under Nick's chin with terrific force. It would have killed a lesser man, snapped his neck like a chicken's. As it was, it lifted Nick a few inches off the sand. As he fell, the sheriff drew back his right hand and slashed sideways at Nick's bared throat. It was the deadly hand-edge blow to the Adam's apple, delivered with the fingers locked into a blade.

The death blow.

Nick swore at himself even as he felt his head exploding and saw the coruscating lights dance through his consciousness . . . and die.

Chapter 5

"Goin' to have me some fun. Goin' to cut it right off the lousy bastard!"

For a moment there was nothing but absolute blackness and the whining drawl of the man's voice. Then the feel of hands groping roughly at Nick's midsection, pulling, gathering. He felt a cold, sharp edge of metal and his eyes flew open.

Dimly he saw the dark, hatchet-faced man squatting over him, a long, ugly blade flashing in the moonlight. The sheriff stood behind him, holding the girl. Nick willed his body to move. It did—but sluggishly. The Seminole parried the blow, slapping his arm back down with contemptuous ease. He laughed, lips drawn back over his wolfish teeth as if he actually meant to bite into Nick's flesh.

"Goodbody!" The sheriff's voice was like a whip. "You all cut that out, hear? We got no time for nonsense. You take little Missy here home in her car. I'll pick you up later."

Deputy Goodbody's voice was incredulous. "You seen what that stinkin' bastard done to her?"

The sheriff was standing over Nick now. "She didn't seem to mind none," he chuckled. "Now hand over the knife." Goodbody did, and the sheriff slipped it back into the sheath that hung from his belt.

So they'd been there the whole time! It had to be the girl herself who'd tipped them off. How else would they have known where to wait? The exhibitionistic little bitch!

"You better get some clothes on, son," said the sheriff affably. Nick found it difficult to move. Everything seemed

36

twice as heavy as usual, seemed to require four times the usual effort. As he pulled on his shirt and pants, Sheriff Grainger said, "Her daddy pays me a bit extra to keep an eye on her. He can't get around much, bein' in a wheelchair." He shook his head, chuckling. "She's a pretty wild one, but we're up to all her tricks. Like usin' this here beach instead of a motel room."

Nick's eyes blazed cold fury, but his limbs felt as if they were weighted down with lead. The sheriff had his hand under Nick's arm now, leading him up the beach with dreamlike slowness. "I guess you always get your kicks first, though, don't you?" Nick sneered through gritted teeth.

The sheriff chuckled. "Wouldn't you?"

Ahead, Nick saw Deputy Goodbody slide behind the wheel of the white two-seater. He was happy to see that Goodbody's right wrist hung limp and useless. At least he'd broken it. If he had it to do over, he would have included the deputy's neck. The girl climbed in the other side of the car, and the two of them roared off across the causeway toward Senior City.

"Now you come along with me, Mr. Reporter," said the sheriff. The patrol car was parked off the side of the highway and camouflaged with branches, but the sheriff led Nick past it to Nick's own battered red sports car. "Get in," he said. Nick did, moving with excruciating slowness. "Slide over," ordered the sheriff. "I'll drive." The car practically sank to the highway under his weight. With a deep, sucking intake of breath, the sheriff squeezed himself behind the wheel, his great hamlike hips flaring out to either side, pinning Nick against the door.

"We could work this up into a pretty good circus act," murmured Nick drowsily. Something hard was jutting into his side. He shifted, trying to get away from it, to get comfortable, to sleep. But no matter how he sat, it continued to press against him. He looked down, saw that it was the handle of the sheriff's knife protruding from its sheath. Some faint memory of action stirred in the depths of Nick's somnolent brain, then vanished. God, if they would only take him some place where he could sleep!

His neck hurt. At first he couldn't remember why. Then

he recollected the hard edge of the sheriff's hand crashing into it. He touched the point of hurt gingerly. His fingers came away wet with blood. The sheriff had pressed the starter and pulled the lever on the steering wheel back into third. The rear wheels now spat sand and gravel as the car roared off the shoulder and onto the road itself, heading toward the causeway.

The sudden motion jogged something in Nick's head. The cool night air streaming around the windshield sharpened his perception. He peered at the sheriff's hand on the wheel, momentarily puzzled by the heavy signet ring on his little finger. That wasn't where one usually wore it. He saw now that it was turned so the intaglio surface was to the side of the finger, in line with the edge of the hand. Of course! he remembered drowsily, he'd used a ring like that himself many times. There would be a tiny, barely visible needle set into the face of the ring, he knew. A miniature hypo. Anyone struck with the ring would receive an injection that acted in seconds, putting the recipient into a gentle trance.

He frowned, struggling to catch the edge of a thought that somehow kept eluding him. The ring. Blood on his neck. Injection. Sleepy. If he could only organize these separate elements into some kind of order. Identification. That would get his thoughts flowing. It came easily, from years of training. Nicholas J. Huntington Carter, Agent N3 of AXE. And this man? A sheriff. He'd been arrested for something. What? Should escape, but don't use knife. Never kill a cop. But, he thought vaguely, cops don't use rings like that. Equipment like that goes with espionage, secret operatives.

And now another thought came swimming lazily toward him. *Sumo* wrestling. This sheriff had been adept at it. Why? A small-town sheriff in the Florida keys—it didn't make sense. Nick finally managed to enunciate the words, to speak them aloud. "You have your *tsuna?*"

The sheriff swung toward him, a wild, lopsided look of mingled surprise and pride on his face. "How do you know about that, son?"

"Watched them wrestle at the *Kodokan*," Nick mumbled.

What had gone wrong with the man's face? The strange

look remained frozen on it. Had he suffered a stroke or something? The features were distorted, bunched obscenely to one side as if swollen by a toothache. They were on the causeway now. The sheriff had turned back, keeping his eyes on the road. "Yeah," he said shortly, "I did some wrestling there, earned my *tsuna*. Army of Occupation. Now you just sit back, son, and don't worry about a thing."

There was something wrong with what he'd just said. Nick struggled to decipher what. His mind was slowly slipping . . . curtains closing . . . one after another . . . *Kodokan*, Tokyo's sacred temple of *Sumo* . . . no foreigner ever allowed to participate there . . . of course, that was it! No foreigner ever allowed to wear the white hemp belt of a grand champion!

Nick took a deep breath and summoned up a last, desperate reserve of strength. His right arm snaked out, the fingers catching beneath the sweaty folds of the fat man's chin. He pulled upward with a decisive jerk. The sheriff's face distorted hideously and came away in Nick's hand—a soft, flexible mask made by experts and worn by a man with blunt Mongolian features and a shiny black topknot of hair!

He lunged at Nick, one hand still on the wheel, the other groping for the knife. Nick's left hand was already on it, securing its grasp. The car careened wildly from side to side, tires screaming as the man's foot bore down on the brakes. Knife out of the sheath now. It was taking forever. The guard rail swung toward them in the glare of headlights. Grating crash of metal as they jerked to one side, glancing off it, swinging across the center line toward the other rail.

The fist with the long steel fingers, and all of Nick's fading strength behind it, lunged upward, through the immense, jerking belly, into the lungs. A shrill sound of surprise and anger burst from the man's lips. His other hand lifted away from the wheel, groping for Nick in slow agony. The terrible face, its eyes shining violet in the glow of the dashboard, sank slowly down, its violet teeth bared, snapping at Nick's hands like a dog. . . .

Nick had the door open. He pulled himself free, felt his shoulder smash into the tarmac. He kicked out blindly, freeing his feet from their hurtling prison. He went spinning along the highway, the world exploding in his head. The red car smashed through the guard rail ahead, turning over and over in grotesque flight. He saw the fat, flying figure of the sheriff, his arms and legs spreadeagled as he soared out of the driver's seat and into the water ahead of the machine. Then he was blotted from sight by the car itself. It sank immediately, leaving only a momentary froth of white on the still, dark surface.

Nick started back along the causeway, limping, his left hand on the guard rail for leverage, pulling himself along. *Keep moving!* he willed his flagging brain. Only a hundred yards to go. Don't stop! Don't get caught on the causeway! He stumbled and fell—and didn't have the strength, or will, to pick himself up. He lay there in the darkness, thinking, *later*. *It's comfortable here*.

Then he heard the distant sound of a motor and was on his feet again, the sweat pouring down his face. He stumbled on with increasing speed. The sound grew closer. Car headlights picked him out of the darkness, pinning him in their glare like an insect on the black felt of a display case. Nick struggled on. In his mind's eye he saw the painted-over fender, and a body sprawled brokenly across the center line.

He was at the end of the causeway. The shoulder of the highway broadened out, sloping away to a dense stand of scraggly pines which merged with mangrove at the water's edge. He plunged down toward their cover, slipping and sliding on the loose gravel. The car was right behind him now. Nick glanced back. It was a blue Oldsmobile, not the white two-seater. As it swept by, he saw the curious faces of an elderly couple peering out at him.

Nick didn't stop, though. He windmilled his way through dry, snapping branches until he was unable to take another step. Then he fell to the ground and let the darkness sweep over him. . . .

The roar of motors brought Nick struggling back to consciousness. His eyes snapped open, then blinked shut again, momentarily blinded by the glare of light. He whiplashed his body to one side, reaching for the gun that wasn't there—and found himself entangled in branches. Through the screen of dessicated pines he could make out water, sky, the causeway. And the motors—those of a deep-sea fishing boat just emerging from beneath the screen, the two tall antennae of her 12-foot rods streaming their lines astern. A fast motorboat came hammering by, close inshore, the water skier on the line behind executing tight slaloms across the waves of her wake.

Nick took a deep breath and struggled to his feet. It was a sparkling, beautiful day. The only jarring note was the twisted, broken stanchions of the causeway's guard rail. They proved that the events of the night before had happened, not been just a nightmare. In which case, what about the sensation he had of the hatchet-faced Seminole returning and asking questions? Was it nightmare or reality? Even now, as he closed his eyes against the painful glare of sunlight on water, he could see the yellowish wolf teeth grinning above him in the darkness.

Nick ran his hands up and down his body. Except for a throbbing neck and what felt like a torn ligament in his right shoulder, he was in one piece. He doubted that he would have been had Deputy Goodbody actually returned. And yet, as he struggled back up the gravel slope, the impression grew. A nasty shock awaited him on the highway. The patrol car was gone. Somebody had come back and gotten it. And *if* somebody had come back, wouldn't they have searched the surrounding underbrush, knowing that he must still be there? And *if* they had found him, wouldn't they have questioned him? And *if* he had been interrogated, had he talked? And *if* he had talked, how much had he told?

The questions plagued Nick every step of the long, sore-footed walk to the Overseas Highway. There was no point in going back to Big Pine. Last night's events had blown his usefulness there, perhaps even his cover. What he had to do now was get back to Miami and contact Hawk.

Nick flagged down a Key West-bound milk truck on the Torch Viaduct and, posing as a stranded motorist, talked the driver into giving him a lift as far as Little Torch. There, he boarded the Miami bus at the local Trailways station. The three-hour journey gave Nick a chance to

sort out his thoughts and to assemble them in the briefest, most concise form for transmission to AXE headquarters in Washington.

He got off the bus just outside Coral Gables and took a
cab to South Miami. There, he wandered about the palm-
lined campus of the University of Miami in seemingly
aimless fashion for a few minutes. Then, certain that he
had not been followed, he boarded another bus for Coconut Grove.

The precautions were a waste of time.

Somebody had already visited Benson's apartment.

Nick stared at the wreckage. The closet door hung open
on one hinge, its contents spilled out like Fibber Mc-
Gee's. The desk drawers looked as if they had been attacked by a hurricane. Benson's suitcases had been torn
apart; even the mattress had been slashed open. Every
single item that bore on the personality and profession of
"Charles Mackley" had been thoroughly examined, and
a casual glance at some of the credentials which had been
unearthed established that "Mackley" had led, in turn,
to Benson.

And what about Nick Carter?

He quickly locked the door behind him and crossed to
the built-in air-conditioning unit. A few quick turns with
a screwdriver and the grillwork came away. Inside, its
purposely dusty surface unblemished by prints, nestled
Oscar Johnson, the only link in the apartment to Agent
N3 and AXE.

Nick breathed a sigh of relief. He had obviously talked
—that injection from the sheriff's ring must have contained some scopolaminelike substance. But the intense
psychological training Nick had undergone at the hands
of AXE's headshrinkers had paid off. He had *not* broken
his cover. He had given facts related only to "Charles
Mackley."

As he activated the short-wave radio, Nick glanced
around the room once again. Something about it bothered
him. A faint sweetish odor mixed in with the almost unbelievable staleness. It was very faint, barely noticeable.
But Nick had smelled it too often in his career not to recognize it immediately. Blood! And with that realization,
the jumble of debris began to assume a definite pattern.

This room hadn't just been searched, he suddenly realized. There had been a violent struggle in it.

Then there was no more time to think about it. The go-ahead signal blinked. Hawk was standing by, waiting for his report.

It took Nick about six minutes to outline the situation in detail. He concluded by saying, "I'm getting rid of Mackley. He's hot."

A series of meaningless vibrations flashed through the airwaves from Washington and emerged from the complex unscrambling machinery of the receiving set as Hawk's voice. "Correction," said the head of AXE dryly. "Not hot, dead."

Nick's brow furrowed. He requested amplification.

"Happened earlier this morning," Hawk's voice said. "Friend Benson apparently hoped to regain favor with his CIA superiors by rigging up a homemade electronic warning device that would go off if anyone searched his old apartment. Completely unauthorized, of course. Anyway, Benson was on duty in the Miami communications room when it went off. He rushed straight to the apartment. They went after him, but it was too late. He was shot through the head. He must have surprised whoever was searching the place, but was overpowered. The searcher—or searchers—got away before the other agents arrived."

Nick felt a brief flash of pity for Benson, then brushed it away. Pity didn't go in this business. Still, the speed and thoroughness with which Benson's body had been removed by his fellow agents was in itself a kind of humiliating epitaph to a hapless career. It seemed almost a denial by the CIA that a man named Ralph Benson had ever lived, or breathed, or walked this earth.

As usual, Hawk seemed to read his thoughts. "There's no time for regret, N3." The voice crackled with urgency. "Discard your cover and leave the apartment immediately. This case has become even more critical than since we last talked. There's a private rest home in Surfside called The Sea View. It's been checked out thoroughly. You're to go to ground there and wait to be contacted. Don't make a move until you are. This is vitally important. Am I understood?"

Nick said he was and quietly broke contact. There was no time to say more. From the door came a soft swishing sound of something—celluloid, probably—sliding past the lock.

Chapter 6

The door swung open with a faint, creaking sigh. Soft-heeled shoes came slowly, silently into the room. Nick gave them just half the time they needed to step to the far side of the doorway, then snaked out one long, agile leg, and one long, muscular arm. The scrawny figure yelped with surprise and alarm. His feet shot out beneath him and his gun pointed ceilingward for one useless moment before clattering to the floor.

It was hard to know who was more surprised—Nick or the intruder.

Captain Clegg's rheumy eyes bugged out at Nick as if he'd seen a ghost. "You!" he croaked. "What's goin' on? I just. . . ."

"Shot me?" Nick's mouth smiled, but a shark swirled and turned in the depths of his cold gray eyes. The other man shivered at what he saw. His hands darted toward his pants pocket. Nick said: "I was hoping you'd try that." His steel-hard fingers closed over Clegg's wrist. Thumb and forefinger pressed. It snapped like a chicken bone. The man howled, hugging the useless appendage to his chest. Nick's hand reached into Clegg's pocket. It was one of those extra-long utility pockets that fisherman favor—and so was the knife inside.

Clegg was the last person Nick had expected to come through the door. Even after he'd watched him run to Sheriff Grainger, instinct had told Nick that the charter captain was just following the sheriff's orders, reporting anyone asking about the hit-and-run. Now he wondered. Perhaps there had never even been such an accident. Maybe Ingra Brand had not been involved. He only had

45

Clegg's word, after all. Perhaps Clegg had lied about everything.

The knife would have to find out.

"Here we go again," said Nick, testing its sharpness.

This was really a job for a delicate stiletto like Hugo, but Hugo was in Washington with the rest of N3's armaments. So a dull-edged fish knife would have to ask the questions. It would be messy, but Nick had no choice. This time he would have to go all the way.

He flipped Clegg onto his stomach and slashed at his shirt, ripping it down the back without being too careful of the pimpled flesh beneath it. Clegg babbled incoherently. Nick had the feeling that this was no act. The man was absolutely terrified. He had an extremely low threshold of pain. Nick was sure he would get the truth—and fast.

The knife bit into Clegg's knotted shoulder as Nick asked: "Did you invent that story about the hit-and-run?"

"No, I swear it, it was just like I said," gasped Clegg, writhing beneath the knife. "I seen the girl hit him an' drive away. Grainger never told me not to tell how it happened, just to let him know if anyone came around askin'. I did. He told me he'd give me a hundred bucks if I told him."

The knife jabbed again, a little deeper. Clegg yelped. "I swear it," he gasped. "Just take the knife away. I'll tell you everythin'. I'm in over my head. I want out, but Grainger won't let me. Every time, there's somethin' more I got to do. I'm scared of that creep. He said he'd kill me if I didn't cooperate."

The knife bit and twisted, withdrew, and briskly pierced the lower back, its curved point hooking into raw flesh. Over Clegg's unintelligible sounds, Nick said: "You better be telling me the truth, because if you're not, I'll kill you myself—only more slowly. Now, tell me everything you know about Sheriff Grainger."

"He ain't actually a real sheriff," panted Clegg, sweat bubbling up at the back of his neck. "More like a private cop. Atchinson hired him for Senior City. He's been workin' there about six months."

"Atchinson?" Nick was surprised.

"Yeah, he calls all the tunes on Big Pine," groaned Clegg.

"And what about Grainger's deputy, Goodbody?"

"He's waitin' downstairs," gasped Clegg, and there was suddenly hope in his voice. "Yeah, you better let me go or he'll be up here!"

The knife made a slow, neat zigzag just below the left shoulderblade. Blood oozed from it. There was no time for subtlety. Nick waited until Clegg's yelps had subsided, then asked what he was doing in Miami.

"He made me come with him. To search your place."

The knife bit even more deeply this time. "You killed a man you thought was me, didn't you?"

Clegg shook his head. "Not me, I swear! He did it."

"Why did he send you back up here?"

"To check something—on the body."

Nick froze. His built-in warning system jangled.

It was too late. From the direction of the door came a sharp click. The side of Clegg's face flew apart like a burst tomato. Nick spun to the right, knife in hand, twisting up from one knee. Through the half-open door he saw Deputy Goodbody. There was a gun in his good hand. It ended in a thick black cylinder. The Seminole grinned his yellowish, dog-toothed smile as the silencer swung toward Nick. The gun clicked again. Hot fire stabbed through Nick's shoulder. He threw the fish knife—less to kill than to distract.

It did, long enough for Nick to reach Goodbody in three great lunging strides. His knee thrust forward and twisted into the lean, sinewy gut. He brought his arm down in a karate chop that shattered the man's wrist. The gun clattered to the floor. But Goodbody managed to slam a ramrod finger blow against Nick's throat with his other hand—the one in the splint. Nick gagged, red pinpoints sputtering before his eyes. Hs was aware of being tossed aside and fallen upon by a snarling beast of a man and pounded brutally against the tile floor of the hallway.

He let himself go absolutely limp for one deceptive moment. Then he jerked his knees up suddenly and heaved with all his strength. The weight flew off him. Nick jack-knifed to his feet, anger balling up inside him like cat's fur. Goodbody was up, too. A blade flicked out from the splint.

Nick caught the outstretched arm, kicked out savagely
with his right foot, and twisted the deputy's trapped arm
until the denim-covered elbow bent up at a hideously unnatural angle toward the face, the tip of the switchblade
pressed against Goodbody's own throat.

"Talk!" The word was like a pistol shot.

Goodbody grinned up at Nick, but there was sickness
in his eyes. He jerked his head savagely to the right, im-
paling himself on his own switchblade. It was expertly
done. It punctured the jugular. Blood spurted from around
the blade as the man pressed himself against the knife
that was killing him, pushing it farther and farther into
his throat. The yellow, doglike teeth clamped together for
the last time. Goodbody sucked in a final, painful gasp of
air. Then his knees folded and he dropped.

Nick dragged him into the apartment by the feet and
laid him out next to Clegg. He locked the door and
searched the two bodies. There was nothing on either
of them. Not even a mask. Their faces were their own.
But as Nick stared at Goodbody he wondered if his features were *really* those of a Seminole Indian. They could
just as easily be Chinese! And why hadn't Goodbody
killed him, out in the keys? He'd had ample opportunity. And another thing—what had Clegg been sent back
to search for on Benson's body? Wait a minute, thought
Nick—*his* body! Because that, of course, was whose body
they had actually thought it was.

With a sudden stab of alarm, Nick stripped off his
clothes. It took him less than a minute to find the tiny
puncture mark the needle had made.

The murmur of voices grew more distinct. A hand
clasped his wrist, feeling for his pulse. Nick opened his
eyes to dazzling whiteness. Part of the whiteness detached itself from the rest and leaned toward him. A
woman's voice, close to his face, said: "He's coming
around, Doctor."

"Thank you, Miss Lyons," replied a male voice. "As I
was saying, Mr. Byrd, there will be no structural damage.
They're doing this type of operation more and more.
Opening up the patient, pumping all his blood out, running
it through the filter and back into him again. It's the filter

itself, of course, that's so remarkable. It passes the blood through but screens out the diseased cells."

"Ah, yes, very efficacious, I'm sure," coughed a dry voice Nick Carter knew as well as his own. He shifted his head slightly to the right—to see a very uncomfortable Hawk perched beside the bed, holding a bouquet of flowers. Even in his weakened condition, Nick couldn't suppress a grin at the incongruous sight. The leathery old man rewarded him with his frostiest smile. "Could someone please take these from me," he said, glancing distastefully at the flowers.

"Yes, the nurse will take care of them," soothed the doctor. He snapped his fingers. "Miss Lyons, see that Mr. Byrd and the patient are not disturbed for the next few minutes. I'm sure they have many things to talk about."

It was all coming back to Nick now as the anaesthetic wore off—how he had found the puncture mark in his arm, radioed AXE and been told to check immediately into the Surfside Nursing Home, which was actually a top-security CIA medical center. The rest was vague, though. He remembered extensive tests, Hawk's arrival, talk of blood transfusions, an operation.

"How long have I been here altogether?" he asked.

"Three days," replied Hawk.

Nick's eyebrows rose in surprise. He tried to sit up. Hawk said: "Might as well relax. You can't leave until tomorrow. And even after that there will have to be two more days of complete rest, then some more tests to make sure they've filtered it all out of you."

Nick asked with some interest *what* exactly it was they had filtered out. "Our people call it X-L Fluid," Hawk replied, with the slightly pedantic tone he always assumed when introducing the latest weapon in the well-equipped spy's arsenal. "A substance similar to Polonium 210. When introduced in the subject's bloodstream it acts as a shield off which alpha particles bounce, thereby pinpointing the subject's location in a manner similar to radar. Instead of a screen, however, a receiving apparatus very much like a Geiger counter is employed. When the subject is approached, the signals become more intense; with each mile of distance placed between the subject and the receiver they become weaker. When an

R.D.F. is used the subject's location can be precisely pinpointed. It works within a twenty-five-mile radius, although they're now experimenting with a fluid that will function accurately within a hundred-mile radius."

Nick whistled softly. "A walking target!" he said. "No wonder they didn't kill me." Hawk began to fidget in his chair. Nick knew what was bothering him. "Go ahead, I don't mind," he chuckled, "and I'm sure the nurse won't care."

Gratefully, Hawk slid a cigar from his vest pocket and bit off the end. "We knew the Russians had their own version of the fluid," he said, striking a match on the sole of his shoe, "but it looks now as if CLAW has it, too." He paused. "I don't want to say too much more to you here," he continued. "The CIA insists security is tight, but as we haven't had a chance to check it ourselves, I'll find other ways of communicating with you in the next day or so."

Both men were silent for a moment—one busily stoking at his cigar, the other recollecting other times he had been pitted against Judas, the arch-criminal of CLAW, Red China's Special Branch in charge of sowing hatred, murder, and the seeds of war.

"By the way," said Hawk, releasing a cloud of bluish-black smoke which almost choked Nick, "we've pretty well determined that the man called Clegg was legitimate. We can account for his background all the way back to birth. He was simply a greedy, conniving type who got in over his head."

"And Goodbody?"

"Both he and Sheriff Grainger would appear to have been born within the last year," said Hawk. He rifled through his pockets. "I have a photograph here that will explain quite a lot."

"But what I can't figure out is what brought Goodbody and Clegg back to Benson's apartment a second time."

"That puzzled us also," said Hawk, "until we found the X-L receiving set in Goodbody's car. We've pieced their movements together this way: They drove to Miami to search Benson's apartment, were surprised by him in the act and killed him, then fled. On their way back to the keys we surmise that they passed the bus in which you were traveling, and that the receiving set reacted violently, at which point they began to suspect that the man they had killed was not you. They thereupon returned to Miami to check the body. The rest you know."

Nick studied the glossy print that Hawk had handed him. It was an aerial view of a scattered string of small islands. "Looks like the Florida keys," he said.

"Yes; the Pine group, to be exact," said Hawk, and handed Nick a scrap of tracing paper on which the outlines of each key had been drawn in ink. "This is a tracing of the *actual* islands, drawn from a photograph taken at the same altitude under the same atmospheric conditions. That outermost one is Peligro. The wavy edge along the top of the paper is Cape Sable in the Everglades, twenty-six miles to the north."

"Actual islands?" said Nick, frowning. "What's this photo of, then?" He placed the tracing over it, noting that the ink lines followed every indentation of the photograph.

"Turn it over," said Hawk.

Nick did. There was some writing on the back. SATELLITE AIR REC PHOTO, he read, TAKEN OVER LAKE KOKO NOR, CHINGHAI PROVINCE, CENTRAL CHINA, SHOWING ARTIFICIAL ISLANDS CONSTRUCTED BETWEEN 3/11 AND 12/6.

Nick glanced up sharply. "Yes, exactly," said Hawk, placing a finger against his lips in warning. "There's even more to it than that. But it will have to wait."

The door had opened. Nick shifted his head, trying to see who had entered, but a screen blocked his view. The nurse's voice said: "I'm afraid you'll have to leave now, Mr. Byrd."

Hawk rose, saying, "Get some rest now, son. I'm heading home but I'll be talking to you soon. I've had some interesting tips on the market in the last few days," he added, as he pocketed the photographs and headed toward the door.

There was a sharp intake of breath from the nurse. "Mr. Byrd!" Nick heard her cry out in a sharp, reprimanding voice. "That filthy, awful old cigar! How could you! It's a wonder you haven't killed the patient! Really, I can't turn my back for a moment!"

A broad grin spread across Nick's face. Everyone at AXE headquarters had felt the same outrage at one time or another at the cheap stogies the old bird insisted on smoking, but none had ever dared vocalize their objections so dramatically. Nick heard Hawk reply testily: "Now, now, Miss Lyons, there's no need to overstress your medical zeal."

The door closed. "Turn over on your side, please," came the nurse's voice, crisp with efficiency. "Face the wall. It's time for your massage." Nick tried to catch a glimpse of her face, but she had her back to him as she crossed to the sink and began running the hot water. He shrugged. A dried-up old battleax, to judge from her voice. He turned gingerly on his side, the dull ache of the shoulder wound returning.

She was at his side now. Off came the covers, down came his pajama pants. With no comment on his scars, she set in, her hands moving in a strong, precise and thoroughly practiced manner. After a few moments she slapped his buttocks sharply. "All right, onto your back!" she commanded.

As he eased himself over, feeling slightly uncomfortable at his nakedness, something hot and wet slammed into his face. Good God! he thought. A hot towel now. Was this absolutely necessary? But he lay back with a sigh, for his body was now bathed in exquisite sensation. The nurse's movements had suddenly lost their professional authority. Her hands were soft, lingering, moving with a gentle rhythm. It was a piercingly luxurious experience, and Nick bathed himself in it. Then all at once he felt the hands shift to his midsection, and what they were doing now was quite unnurselike!

An amazed grin spread across his features. "Why, Miss Lyons!" he chuckled.

Chapter 7

The woman Nick saw as he whipped the hot towel off his face was no dried-up old battleax. Nor was she a nurse named Miss Lyons, though she *was* wearing a nurse's uniform.

As Nick stared at her in amazed disbelief he saw what he had first seen one warm September day in Section 33 of Yankee Stadium and then again aboard a round-the-world jet bound from Bombay to Delhi: soft, copper-tanned skin, high cheekbones, a generous mouth carefully reddened to accentuate its natural beauty, eyes that were almost almond-shaped, rich, dark hair escaping in little curling tendrils from beneath a silly-looking nurse's hat, subtly curving hips, slender waist and, beneath the starched whiteness of her uniform, a high, tilted breastline that evoked all manner of delicious thoughts. And memories.

Nurse Lyons, alias Julia Baron of New York, London and Peking, leaned forward and tenderly kissed him.

Nick's heart glowed as he breathed in the brand of perfume he himself had nicknamed "Dragon Lady." *His* Julie. So seldom seen; so deeply loved. "Julie, baby, sweet baby," he whispered, "let me have another look at you." She straightened up, smiling, showing the slightly crooked teeth that, to him, made her face perfect. "You look as lovely as ever," he grinned, "but hardly my idea of a nurse."

Julie's dreamy cat's eyes glinted with amusement. "Well, that makes us even. Because you don't look very

53

sick, either. Hello, muscles. Hello, scar. Hi, there . . ."
She settled herself on the bed, stroking his great muscles
with her fingertips. "You beautiful monster, what have
you been up to?"

"There's no doubt about it," chuckled Nick. "Your
entrances are getting more and more spectaculàr. But
have you figured out what to do for an encore?"

"Watch," she said and rose, crossed to the door, locked
it, and turned off the overhead light. As she came back
to the bed, her fingers swiftly unbuttoned the nurse's uniform. It slid down her hips to the floor. She stepped out of
it, gloriously, unabashedly naked except for her garter-
belt and nylons. "The head nurse told us to be ready for
any emergency," she said, smiling.

"This is one hospital I think I'm going to like," murmured Nick, taking her in his arms. Her mouth yielded to
his kiss, opened. The tips of two tongues met. His hand
found one of her magnificent breasts, felt it rise and fall
beneath his fingers. He cupped the soft, swelling mound,
then gently squeezed.

"Oh, lovely, my sweet Nick," she murmured, her lips
moving over his face in quick light kisses, brushing his
mouth, his eyelids, the sinewy column of his throat. "It's
been so many months."

"I suppose I should ask what in hell you're doing here,"
whispered Nick, "but I'm almost afraid to find out."

"I'm your bodyguard, honey baby," she breathed into
his ear, "I'm not to let anyone near you while you're
here."

"This is the way to do it, all right," chuckled Nick. And
then there was no longer any time or inclination to talk.
He lifted her onto the bed and pressed the length of himself against her, easing his body into her, and she wel-
comed him, arms spread wide, drawing him close.
There was no competition with her, no battle—just two
magnificent bodies clinging to each other, rocking rhyth-
mically, melding into one, each one concentrating on
the perfect feel of the other as they pistoned the urgent
flames of their twin passions into a single roaring fire.

They whispered endearments which contained hints of
memories of sessions past, and the whispers trailed off
into silence and then increasingly urgent moans escaped

her as she felt the trembling of his body and his intensified drive. She responded with her firm, free-swinging
thighs, until her rose-tipped breasts and the quivering
mound of her dimpled belly became a steady blur of
movement beneath him. And then the black night exploded into red, opened shatteringly beneath them, and
the world dropped away from under their feet. Or so it
seemed to them.

And Nick said, "Julie, *you* I love."

And, as always, he meant it.

Except for the couple stretched out on a large terry-
cloth towel, the beach was deserted. Small waves curled
lazily in across the mirrored water of Biscayne Bay and
broke against the pile of mauve shells which lay at their
feet. Face masks and flippers were at their side. The couple, sunsoaked and flecked with salt, lay in each other's
arms, whispering and laughing. Two martini glasses and
a thermos lay within arm's reach.

They had swum and laughed and made love for the
last two days, and only a few times had they seen any
people anywhere near. The gaudy skyline of Miami
Beach lay along the horizon, but Key Biscayne, although
connected to the mainland by a toll causeway, might as
well have been on another planet. The man raised his
glass, smiled into the girl's eyes and said, "Happy
honeymoon, darling." He drained it and reached for the
thermos. "Oh, oh," he said, holding it to his ear and
shaking it. "Sounds like the honeymoon's over. Still,
it was keen of Dad to have sent it."

The thermos had come in a special-delivery package
that morning, addressed to "Mr. and Mrs. Finch, Key
Colony House, Key Biscayne," and the desk clerk of the
ultra-exclusive resort had rushed it, per instructions, to
the young honeymooners, had received his tip and heard
Mrs. Finch exclaim, "Oh, how delightful! It's one of
those self-cooling thermos units!" And Mr. Finch had
said, "Just the thing for an outing. I'll have the bar mix
up a batch of vodka martinis."

Now the clean-cut young newlyweds lay on the beach,
staring gravely at the thermos. "Shall we?" murmured
Mr. Finch, and his bride nodded. He slid a small, notched

metal plate out of its cap and inserted it into the tiny cooling unit in its base. Then, sitting close to each other and facing in opposite directions, they listened as something inside the thermos whirred slowly and then picked up speed. A thin, metallic voice began rasping softly at them. Though remote and lacking in inflection, its identity was unmistakable. It was no genie, but Hawk who spoke to "Mr. and Mrs. Finch," alias Nick Carter and Julie Baron.

"Now listen carefully," said the voice. "This tape is self-destructive on completion of its cycle and I will relay the information only once. Are you ready?"

As Hawk began the countdown from ten, Nick glanced at Julie and she signaled with her eyes that the beach was empty in her direction.

". . . now, item: Satellite Air Rec photo of artificial islands built in Lake Koko Nor, in Chinghai Province. I won't cover this in great detail as I'm sure Julie already has. Suffice it to say that it was her unit of the O.C.I. which reported the existence of a Red Chinese training school which has been turning out dozens of English-speaking agents who can pass as U.S. citizens. Furthermore, her unit reported the existence of an exact replica of a U.S. town somewhere in Chinghai. This resulted in Air Rec photographing the province and thus discovering the string of artificial islands. Unfortunately, we can't get in any closer than the photograph I showed you. The magnification breaks up beyond this point, due to atmospheric conditions. I'll eat my hat, however, if the replica town isn't on one of those artificial islands."

Nick listened, fascinated. He would eat a couple of hats himself if the town it was a replica of wasn't Big Pine!

"Item: Ingra Brand. In checking her out we unearthed a NASA project so secret that even AXE had not been informed of its existence." Nick smiled at the brief note of petulance in Hawk's metallic voice. "Other than the scientists directly involved in it, only the President and the Joint Chiefs of Staff know about it. It's at Cape Sable in the Everglades. The most powerful, compact atomic missile ever built is being assembled there. It's so powerful, I might add, that whoever controls it can dictate terms to the rest of the world—and that includes the

USSR." The voice paused significantly. "The project is known by the code initials PHO, which stand for Pay-hay-okee, the Seminole name for the Everglades."

Nick's dark eyebrows rose in surprise. So *that* was the information Ochoa had been trying to communicate!

Hawk said: "I'll deal with Ingra Brand's role in the PHO project in a moment, but first I want to clear some other items out of the way. We have run exhaustive checks on her father, on A. K. Atchinson, Aquacity and Dr. Karl Orff. Here, briefly, are the relevant facts. I'll begin with Orff. He's fifty-four, born in Prague, a Sudeten German, left Europe as a DP at war's close, practiced medicine first in the Dominican Republic, then Cuba. A highly skilled surgeon, I'm told. Left Cuba shortly after Castro took power, practiced in Miami. Became a U.S. citizen three years ago. He's semiretired now. Lives in Senior City, spends most of his time fishing, but occasionally sees a few patients on a sort of unofficial basis. One of them is Professor Gunther Brand, who suffered a stroke about a year ago."

Nick lit a cigarette and glanced along the beach. It was still deserted. He turned to Julie. She winked "O.K." They both smiled, leaned toward each other and kissed —the happy honeymooners still, just in case a pair of powerful binoculars was focused on them. The rasping sound of Hawk's voice went on trickling into their ears.

"The relevant facts on Professor Brand are pretty widely known because of the role he played in the development of the atomic submarine. Generally forgotten amid all the praise and publicity he received for that, however, is the fact that he was once Hitler's top underwater idea man, inventor of the snorkel, the two-man sub, and of an under-the-Channel invasion plan of England which never got beyond the drawing-board stage. Apparently even Hitler considered it too outlandish. After the war, Brand was cleared at Nuremberg and hastily rushed to this country, where his background was played down. Frankly, we needed his considerable talents, and he was presented to the public as a 'good, anti-Nazi German.' What his real views are we don't know. He's a tight-mouthed type who says little. The innumerable security checks run on him over the years reveal, however, a basically apolitical type interested only in securing financing for underwater Scientific projects."

Hawk's voice paused while the tape whirred, then continued: "That's primarily why he chose Senior City for retirement. Apparently A. K. Atchinson has turned to him from time to time for advice and help on Aquacity. He's paid a modest retainer by Atchinson's corporation for these services, and lives rent free in Senior City.

"Now, as to A. K. Atchinson himself," the tiny, metallic voice continued, "we've not been able to turn up anything on him that isn't already pretty well known. Self-made Texas oil millionaire now in his mid-sixties. A remote, rather lonely man who hates publicity of any kind. Lifelong bachelor, but with, well, what one might describe as a consuming interest in the opposite sex. Usually has what amounts to a harem of starlets, models and showgirls near at hand. Built his villa on Peligro Key primarily so as to be able to live his satyrlike existence without interference from outraged moralists. Not politically active. The official explanation of why he decided to build Aquacity was that his offshore oil wells got him interested in the possibility of entire communities being established under the sea. Our own investigation, however, has revealed a slightly different motivation."

Nick's ears pricked up. He leaned closer to the talking thermos, exhaling cigarette smoke.

"Atchinson's present mistress," rasped the metallic voice, "or at least his present favorite, is Kara Kane, a former Miami aquatic ballet star fallen on hard times. It's actually for her that the old goat is building Aquacity. She will star in its underwater theater, train her own special swimming corps de ballet, reign as hostess of the underwater hotel and restaurant, and her own line of products will be pushed exclusively in the skin-diving center.

"Now, about Aquacity itself," the voice continued. "Our investigations have turned up nothing that's in the least suspicious. A preliminary permit for a thirty-five million dollar development of the waters off Peligro was awarded to Aquaco—that's Atchinson's corporation—by the Keys Progress Commission. Aquaco will be given three years to complete the development to the commission's satisfaction, after which a thirty-year permit will be issued them. A number of top U.S. manufacturers are contributing materials—aluminum, glass, special tubing. Aquacity will serve as a showplace, apparently, for their underwater products. There have been complaints from the press, of course, about the excessive security precautions surrounding a purely commercial exploit, but that's the way Atchinson always operates. He's on record as having said he doesn't want any damn reporters nosing around, that the public will see what he's built only when it's completed."

Nick scowled thoughtfully. The super-secret Cape Sable project was only 26 miles across Florida Bay from the equally secret Aquacity project! If any two secret projects ever needed investigating, he thought grimly . . .

"Now here are the relevant facts concerning Ingra Brand," rasped Hawk's metallic voice. "She's twenty-six years old, born in Germany. Her mother was killed in an air raid on Hamburg in 1943. She came to this country with her father after the war, was given automatic citizenship which enabled her to live with him in the various government bases at which he was employed. She's an extremely brilliant scientist, highly respected in her field, which is electronic circuit engineering. I'm told she has almost singlehandedly designed the digital and analog electronic circuits on the PHO missile's brain at Cape Sable. She also developed the metal alloy used in these circuits. Brandinium, it's called, in honor of her—an alloy of hafnium and tantalum which can withstand temperatures as high as four thousand degrees."

Nick whistled softly as he tried to connect the brilliant scientist Hawk was describing with the lovely, super-sexed blonde with whom he'd writhed on the beach that night. He was unsuccessful.

"I'm not satisfied with any of this, of course," Hawk's voice continued, "and I'm sure you're not, either. We're going to check and recheck on Ingra Brand. The security chief at Cape Sable seemed reluctant to say more than that she was on extended rest leave at present. I imagine he resents prying by other government agencies. So we'll have to go around him. We've already arranged to have Julie assigned to Cape Sable as a clerical worker from the NASA pool. In that capacity she will have ample opportunity to check all security records.

"It has been further arranged," said Hawk, "that you, N3, will also visit the Cape Sable installation. Your cover will be that of a senior security officer from Washington on inspection tour. Your orders, signed by the Joint Chiefs of Staff, will arrive by special courier within the hour. They will be delivered personally into your hands at the hospital to which you will now return for your final medical checkup. The courier, I might add, is Graham of Editing, and he will have with him all the necessary changes of clothes, personality and documents."

Hawk's voice paused, then continued: "I want you to check every inch of the Sable installation and see if anything—even a cockroach—can get in or out. Make copious notes on any holes in security which you might encounter. Now you'll only have a day in which to do this, so you'll have to work fast. You must be in and out before someone decides to call NASA headquarters to double-check your credentials. That could prove embarrassing.

"When you leave the installation in your official car," said Hawk, "there will be a gray Mercedes parked along the side of State 27 halfway between Flamingo and Homestead. Keep your eyes open for it. At your approach it will start up and you will follow it to a certain gas station in Homestead. In the rest room of same you will hand over your notes, your clothes and the face mask you'll be wearing to the other driver. You will then exchange automobiles, and you will continue in the Mercedes to the town of Everglades on the Gulf Coast, where a team from Editing is at present remodeling a cabin cruiser for your use. You will then proceed to Big Pine Key as Neill Crawford, millionaire sports fisherman and skin-diving enthusiast. Further details on your cover identity, plus all your usual equipment, are awaiting you at Everglades."

The voice died away into a faint sizzle of sound.

Nick waited for a moment or two to be sure that the thermos had finished its work. He knew that beneath its glossy silver finish the contents, already erased, were rapidly disintegrating. Then he removed the combination key and tape head without which the device was useless, and shook the gray powder out of the slot and into the ocean.

"A very illuminating batch of martinis," he said, placing the thermos back in the picnic hamper. "And a delightful honeymoon, too, I might add." Julie smiled and, arm in arm, they headed up the beach.

Hawk hadn't told Nick what he was to do in Big Pine. He didn't have to. The reference to his usual equipment had been enough. This time he would be no bungler going out of his way to draw the enemy's fire, but Killmaster himself!

His job: Seek out Judas and his army of CLAW agents and destroy them.

Chapter 8

"Now, when you press this third button on the control panel the forward deck slides back and. . . ."

Four .50-caliber Browning machine guns rose smoothly and silently into position.

Frankie Gennaro beamed with pride. He was Editing's boy genius, and the remodeling job on the luxurious 40-foot sports fisherman in whose control cockpit he and Nick Carter now stood was his finest job to date. A sweating crew of AXE technicians stood under the tarpaulin which screened their handiwork from prying eyes along the Barron River anchorage just outside the city of Everglades. They were grinning, too, despite the suffocating heat, for they knew that they and their boss had done a superb job.

"They can be fired as a unit or singly," Gennaro was saying, "automatically or manually. The battery fire brackets the target and permits no escape. One hundred thousand rounds of ammo are in position. All you have to do is press this next button over." Gennaro reached out his hand to the bank of buttons at his side and touched one. "Now without the key which you will always carry on you," he continued, "none of these little extras function. To anyone prying around the boat on their own, they're simply so many buttons that have jammed. Nothing unusual about that. You know how many gadgets a fifty-thousand-dollar cruiser like this has."

He led Nick back to the engines, saying, "You have the usual complement of such gadgets, plus a few expensive but quite legitimate extras, like a Decca Navigator and echo-sounder which will be invaluable in the kind of shallow, reef-cluttered waters in which you'll be operating." He stopped in front of the ship-to-shore radio. "When you insert your key here," he said, pointing to a barely noticeable slot, "you'll activate Oscar Johnson for direct, shortwave radio-scrambler contact with headquarters."

The man from Editing and Special Effects now opened a hatch and pointed to the engines. "Twin Chrysler 177s," he said, "standard on this size vessel. But beneath them, something else again. A Westinghouse J46-WE-8B turbojet with afterburner that will give you 5000 horsepower thrust. That means a speed of close to 135 mph. I'll show you the button which activates it on the control bank." He led Nick back into the cockpit. "You have to be careful to activate this one first," he said, pointing. "Otherwise you'll just flip over at a speed like that. This lifts the cruiser up and out of the water on foils and brings special stabilizer fins into play."

Nick grinned. "Beautiful, Frankie, beautiful," he said with honest admiration.

"And the final touch," beamed Gennaro, "to discourage pursuit—twin 40mm Bofers, activated by this button, fire from just above the waterline at the stern. Also, you'll have small magnesium charges that roll out from beneath the fishing chairs and explode and burn in water on contact with the enemy's hull."

An hour later, Nick was steering the *Mobile Gal* through the channel toward Indian Key Light and open water. The cabin cruiser's name was another Gennaro touch. Nick's cover identity of Neill Crawford had been carefully devised to mesh with the real-life Crawfords, a wealthy Mobile, Alabama, ship-owning family. But at the same time the turbojet made this a very mobile, fast-moving gal of another type!

By noon, Nick was off Cape Sable. He could see the red-and-white gantry of the missile base rising above the mangroves and Spanish moss. Only yesterday he had been there, checking out the security of the PHO project with painstaking thoroughness. He had been unable to find a single hole. He had written that in his notes to

Hawk, stating: *Do not believe it possible for unauthorized cockroach to enter or leave base.*

He had also checked into the possibility of storming the base from the sea. But the NASA security team had convinced him that that would also be impossible. They had taken him down in a three-man Perry submarine and shown him the electrified fences and thick concrete buffers that sealed off the underwater approach, the scuba teams who patroled its entire length hourly, night and day. Then, on the surface, he'd been shown the heavily armed picket boats that traversed the waters from Ponce de Leon Bay to the Oyster Keys, around the clock.

Nick decided that a final double-check wouldn't hurt. He was some three miles off the coast at present, following the standard 218-degree course for the keys. He shifted the wheel over to 217 degrees. That would bring him gradually closer to Cape Sable.

Almost immediately his radio crackled. A metallic voice said: "LJ/7017, LJ/7017. You're entering a prohibited area. Can you hear me? Change course southward immediately. LJ/7017, *Mobile Gal,* keep clear."

Nick grinned and swung the wheel back on course. They were on the ball, all right! He could imagine the powerful binoculars they must be using, if they could read his name and registration number. As he slowly pulled away from the coast, the radio crackled again: "LJ/7017. LJ/7017. You will be reported for entering a prohibited area and for failing to acknowledge. Over."

Good, thought Nick. You couldn't ask for more, security-wise. As far as he could tell, they had thought of everything. The only weak link in the chain was Ingra Brand. And Julie Baron was inside the NASA base right now, checking her past records. If there was anything to find, Julie would find it. As for Ingra Brand's present and future—N3 was on his way right now to take care of that.

Nick reached Big Pine by midafternoon.

As he passed under the No Name Causeway, he glanced over his shoulder. The stanchions which had been knocked aside by the sheriff's plunging death car had been replaced. N3 gave his weapons a last check. Wilhelmina,

the Luger: in position in the special spring holster inside
his belt. Hugo, the stiletto: in its sheath along his fore-
arm. Pierre, the gas pellet: in his right-hand trouser
pocket.

This was enemy territory he was now entering. It
looked no different than it had before—the marina still
clogged with pleasure craft, the pennants flying in the
breeze, the Sea-Top Hotel rising into the blue, cloudless
sky, its grounds dotted with chairs and tables and red-
and-white striped umbrellas. But how different he felt
about it!

The marina attendant to whom he now threw a line—
was he really the muscular, freckled-faced Florida Conch
he seemed to be? Or was he also an agent of CLAW? The
attendant grabbed the line and made it fast, then took
down a clipboard to which a list was attached. "Lessee,
you-all must be the *Mobil Gal* from Point Clear," he
drawled, naming the resort town on Mobile Bay from
which Nick had supposedly begun his voyage. "Mr. Crawford, ain't it?" He picked up the telephone and called the
front desk, and moments later a couple of panting bell-
hops hove into sight. What a difference money made, Nick
thought wryly, as he followed them up to the hotel. No
sneers this time; just obsequious bows and hushed commands on all sides as he was ushered to his corner suite
on the third floor without even having to go through the
bother of signing the register.

Nick stripped off his clothes and took a shower. Then
he stretched out on the floor and began his yoga exercises. Six hours at the boat's controls had stiffened his
joints and he now bent every controlled effort of muscle,
breath and limb to eradicate the lingering effects. Fifteen
minutes later he sprang to his feet from a prone position
and toweled off the sheen of perspiration that covered his
lithe, tanned body.

After a second shower he left the hotel for a stroll. His
first stop was a newsstand. He bought that week's edition
of the local paper and read every line of it—but found no
mention of Sheriff Grainger's disappearance. Nor of the
deaths in Miami of Deputy Goodbody and Captain Eddie

Clegg. No mention, even, of the disappearance from the Sea-Top of a magazine stringer named Charles Mackley. Strange kind of paper.

Even stranger bartender, he decided a few minutes later, as he sat over a straight bourbon in The Fish Net. He had just asked the man where he could find a Captain Eddie Clegg, that he'd been recommended as one of the best of the local tarpon guides. "You must be thinkin' of another key, mister," said the bartender, looking him calmly in the eye. "Never been anybody by that name on Big Pine."

Nick returned to the hotel, had dinner, sat around the Bamboo Room for a while on the off-chance that Ingra Brand might come sweeping in. When she hadn't by midnight, he went upstairs, climbed into Neill Crawford's bed, and slept like a baby.

Late the following morning, Nick went down to the marina and told the attendant he was going fishing for the rest of the day. Once he was out beyond the causeway, however, he spun the wheel hard right and took the *Mobile Gal* along the deserted, windward shore of No Name Key.

It was time to visit Professor Gunther Brand.

With the aid of the ordnance survey map he'd clipped to the navigation board, Nick quickly found what he was after—the only channel through the shoal waters on this coast. He flipped on the depth-sounder and guided the cruiser in over the hidden coral heads and on through the mirror-smooth waters of the sheltered cove. The channel was man-made. Flagler or some other early Florida millionaire had built his home in this cove. The ruins of the boathouse were all that was left standing. The rest had been swept away by the hurricane of '35. A sandy, rutted track ran along the shoreline and up, over a low hill, heading—according to the chart—across No Name Key to Senior City.

It would have been a lot easier to rent a car and drive across the causeway. But Nick was pretty sure that it was under 24-hour surveillance—and the element of surprise was vital to the success of this visit. He had a strong suspicion that Professor Brand would be unable to receive him if forewarned of his coming.

Nick anchored the cruiser in deep water, slipped the key from around his neck and inserted it in a tiny slot under one of the bunks. What had looked like solid flooring slid open, revealing 35mm cameras, developers, photographic papers, equipment for making microdots, a high-powered microscope, a box containing passports and credentials, another filled with makeup and masks. This was his Pandora's Box, or Peebee for short—nickname courtesy Frankie Gennaro. An entry-proof steel vault in which he was to keep everything unrelated to Neill Crawford.

Moments later Nick dived off the afterdeck in swimtrunks and struck out for shore. In one hand he carried a waterproof bundle. He quickly swam the short distance, waded across a low sandbar and disappeared into the abandoned boathouse.

The gray-haired man in rimless glasses and the baggy, rather formless suit who came hurrying out of the boathouse a moment later bore no resemblance to either Neill Crawford or Nick Carter. He was an older man, possibly in his early fifties, rather heavyset, with a vague, distracted air about him. Dr. Lawrence Piquett had been associated with Professor Brand at the Woods Hole Oceanographic Institute some ten years earlier. He was very eager to see his old colleague and to discuss some modifications that were planned on the Boletho, the two-man undersea research craft that Brand had developed. He'd come all the way from Massachusetts to talk about them, but—notoriously absent-minded as he was—he'd forgotten to let Brand know he was coming.

The cover identity had been arranged by Hawk, and Frankie Gennaro had delivered the dossier, clothes, Lastotex mask and the skin-tight, flesh-colored gloves which would age Nick's hands to the proper degree. The real Dr. Piquett was safely out of the way, working on a secret government project in Hawaii. Nick knew the exact location of 220 K Street. He didn't want to have to stop and ask questions, and had therefore thoroughly familiarized himself with the gridwork of streets on the ordnance map. A good thing he'd done so, he realized now as he glanced around at the look-alike houses that lined the look-alike streets. Senior City was right out of the ads that say "Retire in Florida on $250 a month." The houses were geometrical sweeps of stucco and cinder block and glass, ribbed with sundecks and clean curving overhangs, and each one named Casa This or Casa That.

The people watering their lawns beneath the long-bladed coconut palms looked as much alike as the houses. The men were all white-haired or bald, with stringy, collapsed chests and paunches beneath their aloha shirts; the women were uniformly blue-rinsed, and the light gleamed on their glasses as they sat rocking on their sundecks. Nick found it hard to believe that anything menacing could exist in this world of shuffleboard and bridge and letters from children and grandchildren up north. But he moved warily nevertheless, his eyes alert.

His mind was mulling over a coincidence, and Agent N3 did not believe in coincidences. It was the wheelchair that Sheriff Grainger had said Brand was confined to. A wheelchair! Once again the film clip unrolled before his eyes. He saw Judas being helped down the airstairs and lowered into—a wheelchair. Gunther Brand. Judas. The same?

A squat, blunt-faced Cuban in a white *guayabera* answered the door at 220 K Street. He studied Piquett's card, while Nick ran through his absent-minded professor act. The Cuban shook his head, handed him back the card and started to close the door. "Wait!" cried a weak, reedy voice from somewhere inside. "It's an old friend." The Cuban looked uncertain.

Nick took advantage of his momentary hesitation and pushed in past him, crying, "Professor Brand, is that you?"

The man in the wheelchair was *not* Judas. That much was immediately obvious. Judas, believed by some to actually be Martin Bormann, was a "Prussian Ox"—bullet-headed, broad-shouldered, barrel-chested. This man was frail, wasted away, with a weak chin, watery blue eyes and silver-white hair that curled down over his collar. He came wheeling out of the darkened room, his lower lip trembling with—what? Effort? Eagerness? Nick couldn't tell. A malacca cane hung from the back of the chair, suggesting that he could, if necessary, get around without it.

"Old friend! Old friend!" he cried in a quavering voice. "It's been so long. How are you? Tell me all about yourself. What is going on now at the institute? What did you think of the Sealab II experiment?" The questions came tumbling over each other. Suddenly he broke off, glancing past Nick, a quick shadow of fear flitting across his face.

Nick turned. Dr. Orff had just entered the room.

"What is the meaning of this intrusion?" demanded Orff, his eyes bulging furiously from his parboiled doll's face.

Nick started into his act again, but Orff cut him off with an impatient wave of his hand. "Don't you realize that Professor Brand is extremely ill? He suffered a stroke not more than. . . ."

"I suffered a stroke," repeated the man in the wheelchair as if by rote. "I suffered a stroke a year ago, and then another only a few months ago."

Nick stared at him cautiously. There was something very peculiar about the way he had said that. "Well, I had no idea," he said. "You see, I wanted to discuss. . . ."

"Any discussions are best handled by mail," interrupted Orff. "The professor cannot stand excitement. Now, as his personal physician, I must ask. . . ." All at once he broke off, peering at Nick with sudden, heavy-eyed interest. "Your car is outside?"

"No, I came by cab."

Nick caught the quick nudge the Cuban gave Orff. "Strange. I didn't hear one pull up," murmured Orff, placing a gold-tipped cigarette between his lips and lighting it.

"The driver misunderstood me," replied Nick, "and took me to A Street. It was pleasant, so I decided to walk." As he spoke, he kept his eyes on the Cuban. The man had edged around him and was now wheeling the unprotesting professor out of the room. "Wait," said Nick, "I would at least like to say goodbye to my old friend."

Orff gently but insistently guided Nick toward the door. "Quite useless," he murmured, as the smoke curled up around his heavy-lidded frog's eyes. "See, even now he says nothing. My friend, he has already forgotten you." Orff shrugged expressively, his eyes suddenly spaniel-soft with bogus emotion. "His moments of lucidity grow increasingly rare." He made a gentle clucking sound and opened the front door, maneuvering Nick through it.

As the door closed in Nick's protesting face, a car screeched to a stop in front of the house. He whirled around, the hard, pantherlike body beneath his shaggy suit ready for instant action.

Ingra Brand slid out from behind the wheel of her white two-seater and came up the front walk toward him. She was wearing a white bikini, and Nick's seemingly casual glance missed nothing—the narrow waist, the full, rounded hips, the legs graceful and tapering below. She raised her sunglasses as she approached, shaking out her heavy blonde hair.

"Dr. Piquett, isn't it?" she said. "It's been so long, I'm a bit hazy."

After exchanging a few brief pleasantries, she started to brush past him. Nick smiled broadly and tried to prolong the conversation. He had hoped at first that she might invite him in; now he would settle for just another brief glimpse of her face. There was something odd about it, different. She had changed somehow. Not physically perhaps—but definitely changed. "You'll excuse me?" she murmured. "I've come from the beach. I'd like to get out of these wet things."

Nick watched her enter the house. *What was it?* The longer he had looked at her, the more puzzled he'd become. There was something odd about her, but he couldn't put his finger on exactly what. He turned and started away from the house, moving thoughtfully along the sidewalk.

Something so small as to be barely noticeable. Only Nick's trained eyes would have caught it. But it was his attention to the small things that had kept him alive this long—a brand of perfume, the way a woman's ears looked when her hair was up, a nervous little gesture of some kind.

Nick had gone about two blocks when every bell in his warning system began to jangle. He glanced up—and his body tensed.

The whole atmosphere of Senior City had suddenly changed!

Chapter 9

PEEKABOO! I SEE YOU!

Nick stayed in character. He shuffled briskly along, his thoughts apparently a thousand miles away. But every nerve and instinct beneath the rumpled, ill-fitting suit watched, listened. Strove to feel and sense what specifically had changed. What was out there. Who was out there. Around him.

There were no sinister faces peering out of shadows. No shadows, even. It was bright, hot, an hour or so past midday. A slight breeze stirred the royal palms that lined the quiet residential street. People were watering their lawns, gardening, sunning themselves on the sundecks of their neat white houses. Here and there small knots of elderly folk stood chatting.

Yet Nick smelled danger. Its stench was so intense it almost gagged him.

He quickened his step.

The group of white-haired old codgers he had just passed were discussing the stock market and tut-tutting about prices in Big Pine. They hadn't even glanced up as he'd gone by, but something, some extrasensory instinct caused Nick to glance back over his shoulder a moment later.

Two of them had broken away from the others and were following him. Elderly retired types, wearing sunglasses and flowered shirts—but there was nothing elderly about the way they moved along the sidewalk behind him. Their stride was sure and purposeful.

Nick quickened his pace. From the corner of his eye he saw that they did also.

Up ahead, more elderly types. Standing in tight little

groups along the sidewalk, chatting amiably together. Some had newspapers under their arms; others held dogs at the ends of leashes. It all looked innocent enough. Except that Nick's trained eye immediately spotted the pattern. Every hundred-odd yards on alternate sides of the street. There was nothing random about that. Chance could never have positioned them so effectively.

They had him completely sealed in.

There was a time to think, a time to move. Nick had learned how to distinguish one from the other during his brief but bitter apprenticeship. This was a time to move. To let his splendid, yoga-trained body take over even while his mind was still analyzing the problem.

He was already in motion. The ridged rubber shoes with the hard inner lining bit into the gravel of the nearest driveway. Nick sped down it in great lunging strides. Behind him, there were shouts, the sound of running feet. He dodged past the garage, went plunging through a backyard filled with drying sheets, and saw the fence come sweeping toward him. He drew a deep breath, bunched his muscles—and took the fence in one easy, swinging stride, his right arm gripping its edge, giving him extra leverage and balance.

He came down in a flower bed. An elderly woman with a garden trough, her hair in curlers, straightened up from her nasturtiums and screamed. He grinned apologetically, and swept on, wishing he had time to go back and strangle her. For she continued to scream. Her voice went up and up like a siren, zeroing in his position more effectively than any direction finder. Was she also a CLAW agent? Was everyone in Senior City?

He vaulted another fence, then another. His swift, zigzagging course took him down a driveway, across a street, then between two houses and through more backyards. The sounds of pursuit grew fainter. He went on running with his light, loping stride until he came to the Avenue Two Esplanade. He knew from the ordnance map in his head that this would lead him out of Senior City into open country. He slowed to a walk, becoming elderly, graying Dr. Piquett again.

With amazing computerlike speed, Nick's mind was analyzing what must have happened as, simultaneously, he plotted his next moves. Orff and the Cuban could have seized him while he was still in the house and thus have avoided this wild chase. That they hadn't, meant that something or someone had changed their minds about him *after* he'd left the house. What? Who? Ingra Brand? She had known the real Piquett. Had she somehow seen through Nick's cover? And what about the strange behavior of Professor Brand? Nick had seen that kind of repetition by rote before. In the victims of the Chinese thought reform technique known as *Hsi nao*—literally "wash brain." And the change in Ingra Brand? Something, some small detail in her physical appearance had raised a tiny question mark. What was it?

A faint squeal of tires sounded behind Nick. He spun around. A long black hearse had just swung out of a side street into the esplanade. Wilhelmina slid into N3's ready hand, but both remained inside his right-hand trouser pocket. The hearse glided to a stop directly in front of him. Nick's grip tightened around the frame of the stripped-down Luger, then relaxed slightly as the cheery, scrubbed face of a clergyman beamed out at him.

"You're a friend of Professor Brand's, aren't you?" he asked cheerfully, leaning across the seat toward the window on Nick's side. "I'm the Reverend Bertram," he explained. "The chaplain here. I've been trying to catch up with you for three blocks." Nick watched him carefully, saying nothing. The clergyman patted the seat beside him. "I'm heading over to Big Pine," he said. "Care for a lift?"

Something was wrong with it all. How did this clergyman know he was a friend of Brand's? How did he know which street it was that he'd dodged down? Nick glanced quickly up and down the silent, deserted esplanade. There was no noise except the zing of crickets and the soft tickover of the hearse's engine.

The Reverend Bertram said something in a low voice. Nick couldn't hear what. Cautiously he leaned toward the window. "Are you in any kind of difficulty?" the clergyman repeated, his face suddenly grave and concerned. "I saw a number of people running near the professor's house. Is he all right? I tried to visit him after his last stroke, but that strange-looking doctor turned me away. When I saw you come out of the house earlier I thought you might have some news."

Nick studied the clergyman intently. It was hard not to trust the wide blue eyes behind the rimless spectacles, the pink baby's skin, the speck of shaving cream near the earlobe, which somehow completed the perfect picture of otherworldly innocence. But N3 trusted no one.

There was a hint of movement in the rear-view mirror over the Reverend Bertram's head. Nick swiveled his eyes up to it. Two men were approaching along the sidewalk. He spun toward them. Dark glasses, flowered shirts. One tall, the other short and fat. The two oldsters who'd begun the chase! Nick swung the other way. Two more senior citizens were approaching from that direction. They had him boxed in!

"Can I help you?" the Reverend Bertram called out anxiously.

But Nick was already running. A shot slammed past his ear, whanging off the curb ahead of him. He angled sharply to the right and up another driveway, crouching low and twisting as though he were running across a battlefield. Footsteps came pounding after him. Another shot rang out, ploughing up gravel to his left.

Wilhelmina was out and ready. Nick made a sudden leaping turn sideways and fired twice as he jumped. The first of his pursuers clutched at his neck and spun slowly round, falling to the gravel. The other shot was wild. It caromed against a far wall. Behind him a window shot up. Someone screamed. Nick turned and went darting along the edge of a backyard swimming pool. The other gunmen had leaped for cover. This was his chance.

Ahead he saw open country—but between lay a high grillwork fence. Too high to scale. Nick sucked in his breath. His yoga-trained body elongated strangely. The normally broad shoulders became oddly loose and curiously distorted. Even his rib cage seemed to contract. He wormed his narrow hips through the almost-as-narrow opening, landing lightly on his hands in soft dirt. Then he was up and running again. Just in time. Behind him a gun crashed. A bullet whipped past him as he reached the cover of some rocks.

Keeping the rocks between him and his pursuers, he

continued across open country. It would take them a few minutes to scale the fence—enough time for him to reach the marshland directly across the island from where he'd left the boat. From the cover of the mangroves there he would have a chance to see exactly how many of them he was dealing with, and plan accordingly.

Nick ran with a long, loose-legged stride, glancing over his shoulder occasionally. It was very hot out in the open. A harsh, banking wind had sprung up from the south. The glare from the sea and from the shiny green leaves of the mangroves up ahead was dazzling. A smell of marsh gas and guano hung in the air. The first couple of "senior citizens" had gotten over the fence, he saw. Nick picked up speed, dodging through the low scrub and screwpalm that grew in tufts between gray dead coral. The coral itself banked sharply away toward the marsh, providing perfect cover. He dodged down behind it, Wilhelmina ready.

There were three of them altogether, he saw, spread out and coming fast for men supposedly drawing Social Security. They came down the slope, crashing through the low bamboo and sea grape. Now that they'd left Senior City behind they weren't kidding around. Nick saw the big fat one become suddenly thin as he pulled a submachine gun out from under his aloha shirt and discard the kapok filling in which it had been embedded.

But even more surprising, they seemed to have no doubts about where Nick was. The one with the submachine gun pointed it at the exact formation behind which he crouched. There was a swift rattling roar. Fragments of splintered coral whined overhead like hornets. Ricochets twanged and buzzed off into the underbrush. The mangrove bush above him was now being torn to shreds. *Zwip, zwip, zwip,*—as if a scythe were cutting it. Then the noise stopped. Silence. The stench of cordite and the sour smell of blasted coral hung in the air.

Nick raised his head a fraction of an inch. The machine gunner was pulling back the bolt to reload, foolishly standing in the open as he did so. Wilhelmina barked. The bullet skimmed the hairy arm that held the gun and slammed into the aloha shirt. The man's face twisted with the unbelievable pain. He swayed for a long moment, then dropped. Nick was moving even as he fired, darting from behind the coral toward a stand of mangrove.

The second gunman showed himself briefly, rising from behind the coral ledge. His gun spoke with an angry whine as Nick threw himself to the side, fell to one knee, and aimed. Wilhemina exploded into a bark of rage. The other gun fired again—but wildly. Coral chips flew up at Nick's feet. The gunman slumped down out of sight. The third senior citizen had had enough. He went scrambling up the slope like a frightened rabbit. Nick drew a bead on him, then lowered the Luger, thinking better of it.

He edged forward and examined the two men he'd brought down. They were both dead. One glance told Nick the story. Youthful, rugged bodies, the faces of old men—but not masks. That surprised him. The scars near the ears and beneath their hairlines suggested plastic surgery in reverse—an aging process achieved by loosening the skin folds and chemically pitting its surface, creasing it. A permanent, undoubtedly painful process. Who would be so fanatical as to allow that to be done to them? The submachine gun provided the answer. It was a T'su VTL—a Chinese-made imitation of a Russian weapon.

Smearing over his footprints and walking, whenever possible, on seashells and twigs, Nick worked his way up a vast slope toward a kind of low plateau covered over with scrub and rocks and spindly, wind-bent trees. This was the highest point on No Name Key. It commanded a view both of Senior City and the windward shore where the *Mobile Gal* was moored. There was no activity in either place. Nor in the mangrove marshes below, which stretched away toward the dancing heat haze on the horizon.

Nick waited atop the hill the rest of the afternoon, lying flat against the pulverized shells and sea grape, his eyes peeled for the slightest movement. There was none. Apparently no one was going to come after him. Very strange, that.

Under cover of darkness, Nick descended the far side of the slope and took the long way around the deserted eastern end of the island to the cove where he had left the boat. He stopped a number of times to watch and listen. But he was not followed. Before entering the abandoned boathouse to change, he waited for half an hour, crouching in the darkness, eyes peeled for any sign of a trap. Instinct had already told him there was no one about, but he wanted to make doubly sure.

With Dr. Piquett folded up in the waterproof bundle, Nick catfooted his way through the abandoned boathouse and down the rickety steps to the beach. Wilhemina and Pierre were in the bundle also; only Hugo was still strapped to his wrist in its pencil-like sheath.

Suddenly he stopped, aware of an alien sound. Barely audible, almost a vibration—the rolling of a pebble or the crack of a dry twig. He spun around.

Too late. The attack came from above.

A tall, rawboned figure threw himself on Nick from the coral ledge that encircled the boathouse. Nick felt the powerful arms twist his body hideously. Off-balance, he went down, his head slamming against the bottom step. In a red haze of sudden pain and dizziness he saw the big, spatulate fingers reaching for him again.

Nick clawed upward, seeking the soft part of the muscled neck, and felt his own head snap back with a windpipe blow that tore the night apart with bursting light. It had been delivered by a second figure—short, squat, also in flowered shirt and dark glasses. Mutt and Jeff! The two oldsters who'd originally begun the chase! *How had they found him?* It was impossible. He had even switched cover disguises. There was no possible way they could have connected Dr. Piquett with Neill Crawford. And yet they had. And because of that they would have to die.

A shark swirled and turned in the depths of Killmaster's eyes.

Hugo snaked out of its sheath, slicing upward into the second man's belly. He stumbled backward, fell against the bigger one. At the same instant, N3's foot snaked up in a scientifically brutal kick that caused the big fellow to loosen his grip and draw his breath in sharply. He doubled over, hands fumbling toward the source of the unbelievable pain. As he did, a karate-hard hand hit him like a mailed fist on the lower neck. Something snapped.

If Mutt were still alive, he was certainly dead before he hit the ground.

Jeff, meanwhile, had ripped off his dark glasses. Now he came leaping toward Nick with a snarl of animal hatred. Blood was spreading fast across the flowers of his shirt, but there was still terrific power in the squat, heavyset body, and it was backed by the insane rage of a wounded, dying animal. Nick hooked his foot around the man's calf and kicked hard at the knee with his iron-shod heel. The leg snapped, hurling the man forward onto Hugo's gut-biting, icepick blade. Nick jerked the killing steel back out, ready for a second thrust. The young eyes in Jeff's old, wrinkled face glittered with hatred, and again he lunged. Nick spun to one side and struck. Razor-sharp steel sank into the side of the neck like a hot pick into butter.

Nick staggered to his feet, grabbed the waterproof bag and waded out into the water.

The Reverend Bertram sat in the front seat of the hearse, watching through his binoculars as Nick Carter swam toward the *Mobile Gal*. He was parked at the top of the nearby rise, and was wearing earphones. He smiled, reached around and opened the coffin behind him. It was jammed full of complicated wiring and dials and the slowly revolving antenna of a direction finder. The clergyman activated the two-way radio that sat beside it in the coffin and picked up the mike.

"You were right, Orff," he chuckled. "There are still enough traces in his bloodstream to activate the receiver if he's within a two-mile radius. What's that? No, he got away this time. Just killed two more of the K Street guards. That makes five now." His big, innocent blue eyes twinkled merrily behind the rimless glasses as he said: "AXE obviously cares enough to send the very best."

Chapter 10

A WHISPERING TAPE, AN
OLD-FASHIONED RAPE

The celluloid made a soft swishing sound as it slid past the lock. The door inched open, light from the hall streaming into the darkened room. The girl paused in the doorway, her figure silhouetted by it. The rounded supple line of her hips twisted as she slowly closed the door behind her. The sharp outline of her uptilted breasts was the last thing visible.

Then the room was dark again.

She moved through it with complete familiarity, neatly avoiding the big glass-top desk, the battery of files, the conference chairs scattered about. Her heels made no sound in the thick wall-to-wall carpeting, and she slipped her shoes off when she came to the reinforced steel door at the far end of the office.

This one took longer to open. There were two locks on it, one of them a combination type of extremely advanced design.

But there was no lock in the world that could delay Julie Baron more than 15 minutes—and this one was no exception.

She padded silently across the tile floor of the smaller room, moved a chair out from behind a table and slid open a card file. A pencil-thin beam of light sprang from her fist and moved along the cards, stopping at one. She closed the file and moved across the room to a cabinet whose shelves were neatly stacked with spools of electromagnetic tape. Again the beam of light combed them. She slid out a spool and fitted it onto the tape recorder.

Julie's three-day search of the NASA security records at Cape Sable had finally narrowed down to three spools of tape in Dr. Howard Dunlap's office. Dunlap was the project psychiatrist, and every question Security had raised about the increasingly strange behavior of Ingra Brand during the last eight months had been referred to him. His answers, recorded in memos to Security, were invariable:

"Subject's behavior in no way a security risk, but the natural result of strain caused by overwork and the confined conditions under which the scientific community is forced to live while working on Project PHO. A brief respite from the usual routine might be in order; perhaps a visit with the subject's father, as her relationship with him is quite a close one and she seems unduly worried by a stroke that he recently suffered."

All well and good—only Julie hadn't been able to find the typewritten transcript of Dunlap's interviews with Ingra Brand in the files where such interviews belonged. Neither had Major Bessler, Chief of Security, and he had sent a testy memo to Dunlap, who had replied that his office was running behind on paper work, but that the interviews would soon be available for further study by Security. And there the matter had rested.

Until Julie's arrival at Cape Sable.

Her cover job in Personnel Records had placed her right down the hall from Dunlap's office in the main administration building, and the recent arrival of a large team of Guidance, Component and QIE engineers from NASA HQ in Houston had given her a legitimate reason to be in the building until all hours. The rest had simply been a job for her Lockpicker's Special.

A quick preliminary check of Dunlap's office had revealed that he *wasn't* behind in his paper work. A fastidiously neat, hard-working type, he was actually ahead of himself. Ingra's missing interviews therefore stood out like a missing front tooth in a model's smile.

On her second nocturnal visit to his office, Julie had located the missing interviews. They were still on tape, hidden away in the inner recesses of the top-security records room adjoining his office. Last night, Julie had played the first of them.

It had been a real eye-opener.

Tonight she would listen to the second spool and, if there was still time, also the third and last. She felt for the chair in the darkness and sat down, flicking on the recorder. The spools began turning. She leaned forward intently as Dr. Dunlap's soft voice whispered through the room. She had to strain to hear it, but didn't want to risk turning up the volume.

"In our last session," whispered Dr. Dunlap's voice, "you were telling me about this recurring nightmare of bombardment, blood and death by which you say you've been plagued all your life. I've been thinking about it, Ingra, and it seems to me that it somehow stems from your mother's death in that air raid on Hamburg. In those terms it's a perfectly natural occurrence. . . ."

"I don't remember my mother's death," Ingra Brand's voice cut in, tight with suppressed emotion. "I was only two when it happened. In this nightmare I'm always five years old, and the sense of loss I feel is not for my mother but for my sister. . . ."

"Ingra, we've already been over that," replied Dr. Dunlap patiently. "We both know you never had a sister, twin or otherwise. Your father's told you that; the records corroborate it."

"All my life," whispered Ingra, "I've felt this painful sense of loss. So painful it's almost physical. I feel cut in half, incomplete, and I've read somewhere that when a twin dies this is how the surviving one feels."

"There is no twin, though, Ingra. Look at your records. Look at the exhaustive search NASA Security has done on your background over the years. Your life has been checked again and again by a dozen different agencies, because of the sensitive nature of your work. If you were an ordinary citizen, one could entertain the possibility of an unknown sister. But not someone whose life is as fully documented as yours."

The tape whirred on while Dr. Dunlap paused for breath. Then the whispering began once again to trickle into Julie's ear. "Don't you see, it's a projection of one side of your nature. A part with which you have been warring for years; one that demands that you let yourself go."

Ingra's tight, barely controlled whisper now cut in again, saying, "It's been getting worse lately. Barely a night passes that I don't dream of her. I hear her voice calling as the roof collapses, and then I'm running through a river of blood and fire. . . ."

She continued in this vein for a few minutes, then burst into tears, and Dr. Dunlap was saying, "That's all right, go ahead, get it out of your system," in a soothing voice. The tape whirred silently and then Dunlap spoke again, but in a businesslike manner now that suggested he was alone. "Notes on session two," he said briskly. "Subject shows classic symptoms of advanced schizophrenia. Quite severe personality disorientation. . . ." There was a long pause and then, in a barely audible voice, he added: "Perhaps warmth, human affection could break through . . . too severe? I wonder . . . a man who could give her the love she deserves . . . scratch that later. Let's see . . . subject also shows. . . ."

Julie's graceful eyebrows arched with surprise in the darkness. Here was a new note! a fascinating one, too. She *had* to play spool three—and immediately! She flicked on the pencil flashlight and, placing it between her teeth, set about switching spools.

She was so caught up in the task that she didn't notice the widening crack of light in the outer office.

The man eased the door open inch by inch. He had a gun in his hand. He moved silently across the heavy carpeting toward the half-open steel door. He paused as the faint voices on the tape recorder drifted out to him.

"Dr. Dunlap, I've got to tell someone!" Ingra Brand's voice was saying tensely. "Some of the things I told you in the first two sessions were not dreams like I said they were. I mean the parts about my father. That stroke, the people he seems to be involved with ever since he moved to the Florida keys. It's not my imagination. He's really in danger. Grave danger. We all are."

"Don't talk like that, Ingra!" Dr. Dunlap's voice was sharp. "You know that these sessions will eventually find their way into your record. I'm going to go back later and erase what you just said. Your career would be finished if that sort of talk ever got into it. To describe a dream is one thing, to say that you believe it actually happened is another. Ingra, I'm going to be honest with you. You aren't well. You need a rest. A long rest. I'm going to recommend it. After you've rested a few months I'm going to talk to you again, and we'll see what the next step will be. . . ."

"Doctor, I just realized something," said Ingra Brand's voice. "You really think I'm . . . mentally disturbed!"

"Not disturbed. Just overtired, overwrought."

"No, I don't believe that's all. Not for a minute. You think I'm seriously ill. You said yourself that I'd be dropped from the project if these sessions got into my record. So why are you doing it? Why are you taking a chance with your own professional reputation just to save my neck?"

"Not your neck," replied Dr. Dunlap, "a brilliant scientific career." There was a pause, a long one this time, while the tapes whirred. "No, that's not true either," he said with sudden intensity. "You must know by now why I'm doing it, how I feel about you . . . Ingra, I'm in love with you, have been ever since I first met you. . . ."

After a moment Dr. Dunlap's voice continued. But it was not on tape now. It was in the room. It said: "So you've found out my little secret." The overhead light flashed on. Julie whirled around—to find herself blinking into the barrel of a snub-nosed automatic.

Ingra Brand, in black with a square-cut neckline and with one large diamond on a thin chain at her throat, looked morose and bored.

Nick had spotted her the moment he'd entered the Bamboo Room.

The place was crowded with sunburned people in loud, tropical get-ups—brilliant garish shirts, pangling gold bangles, dark glasses with jeweled rims, cute native straw hats—and Ingra's stark, stylish simplicity made her stand out like a sore thumb. A half-finished vodka martini was on the bar before her, and she was fishing around in a silly, oversized handbag as Nick approached. She had the Luckies out and the cigarette in her mouth as his lighter flared.

She glanced up. Nick flashed her his most dazzling millionaire sportsman's smile. "Hello," he said, "my name's Neill Crawford. May I buy you a drink?"

The look she gave him was speculative, appraising. His own eyes marveled at the perfection, the breathtaking beauty of the woman before him. The only jarring note was her handbag, which somehow seemed more suited to a shoplifter. But then Nick had never liked the things anyway. A woman this beautiful should have a servant following her around just to hand her Kleenex, perfume, cigarettes, lipstick, eye shadow and all the other supplies she would need.

There was a blare of brass from the band and a spatter of fingers on the bongos, and then away they went, their scarlet satin calypso shirts jumping in time to a syncopated rendition of "Yum Bambe." Ingra inclined her head slightly. "Drink, no," she said. "Dance, yes."

But her mind seemed not to be on it. She danced well, but without the rapt intensity with which she had danced last time. Nick thought it might be the number, but when the beat changed, and they danced slowly, and she pressed against him, her hips swiveling against his, there was still something slightly off about it. She was far from clumsy, yet there was a certain hesitancy to her movements, a lack of pliancy, as if her body were unconsciously resisting his.

It puzzled Nick. He pulled away slightly and glanced down at her. She smiled up at him through half-closed lids. "It's so crowded and stuffy in here," she murmured. "I feel rather dizzy. Could we step outside a moment?"

She sprang it on him as they leaned against the railing of the balcony, gazing down at the Sea-Top's darkened swimming pool.

"There's a beach I know," she whispered, and, without looking at her, he knew that her lips would be parted and moist, her eyes beguilingly seductive. "No one ever goes there. It's just this side of the No Name Causeway."

So—killing the guards hadn't been enough! There were others who had connected Dr. Piquett with Crawford! And they had sent her to lure him back out. N3's eyes hardened. They hadn't wasted any time about it. He'd done his yoga exercises, showered and grabbed a sandwich on his return from Senior City, then gone downstairs to the Bamboo Room. It had taken him less than an hour, all told—and she was already there, waiting for him. He wondered with grim amusement which approach technique she would have used if he hadn't approached her first. The spilled drink? The stepped-on toe?

His finger came up under the diamond she wore, giving it a casual flick. "Not with that on, honey," he said. "We'd have every jewel thief between here and Miami for company. Besides, I'm expecting an important phone call tonight." He paused, then added with a sly leer, "But take my room, now. It's as lonely and deserted as any beach—and the bed's a lot softer than sand."

She flushed and glanced away. But why make it easy on her? He'd had a crawful of this whole business.

"All right," she murmured, her voice barely audible.

Nick concealed the brief but thorough going-over he gave his third-floor suite, during vague mutterings about making Ingra a drink. No one had been in any of the three rooms since his last search, less than an hour earlier. He patted the large bed that rose like a triple-decker sandwich from the floor. "No legs," he grinned. "Bridal suite. Guess they didn't want to take a chance on its collapsing."

He hurried into the next room, then glanced back out at her. "Do you do this often?" he asked, and saw her flinch. But he didn't care what he did to her now. The game was nearing its conclusion. In less than half an hour she'd be talking her head off, telling him everything he wanted to know.

He snapped open the traveling bar which Editing had provided. A bottle of vermouth and one of vodka were nestled beside each other in the attaché case, together with an aluminum shaker, stirring spoon and two glasses. He took the glasses out and filled them both with vermouth. "I've run out of vodka, I'm afraid," he called out. "Straight vermouth okay?"

The heavy sweetish taste of the vermouth would cover what he was about to put in her glass. He pressed a certain spot near the edge of the case and a tiny metal slot sprang out from what had appeared to be the lining. He heard Ingra say yes, that would be all right, as he slid the top off the slot and took out the capsule. He dropped it into her glass and it immediately dissolved, its colorless contents blending imperceptibly with the vermouth.

Talkalot—that's what Poindexter of Special Effects had dubbed the scopolaminelike substance. Truth serum—guaranteed to make anyone start spilling out his deepest, darkest secrets within 20 minutes. Meanwhile, there'd be sex to keep them busy. And with the mood Nick was now in, it would not be a gentle experience.

How would she react? he wondered grimly. Which of the innumerable erotic types in her repertoire would she play this time?

"No! Not like this!" she cried, as his hand closed around the front of her wispy black bra.

Ingra had drunk the vermouth in one gulp—as if needing its support. And, at his suggestion, she had slipped out of her dress. Now he stood before her, insolently naked and aroused, his eyes cold gray steel. With one motion of his hand, she was naked to the waist, and he pulled her against him without even looking at her. He kissed her brutally. His hands were in her heavy blonde hair, his thumbs under her jawbone, at either side of her face, so that she couldn't twist her face away. He felt her knees give way beneath her, but still he ground his lips into hers, holding her upright with his hands tangled in her hair. His tongue forced an entry through her teeth, then reached deeply, brutally thrusting and ramming, filling her mouth, ignoring her gurgling protest, overwhelming the fluttering defense her own tongue weakly made.

Then he shoved her down onto the bed, ripped the black lace panties off and stood looking down at her. She flinched beneath the ravaging glare of his eyes, and automatically brought her hands up to cover her breasts and the soft golden V of her sex in the classic posture of shamed nudity. He pulled her hands aside brutally, pinning them over her head with one hand as his gaze moved slowly down her body, pausing at the bold thrust of her breasts, sliding around the flare of her hips, lingering over the long, smooth curve of her thighs.

She began to sob, but he ignored her, for he saw her pink nipples stiffen from the exciting stimulation of his hard-eyed stare. So this time she was to be the violated innocent! thought Nick grimly. They would both see how long she could keep that up.

She gasped as his weight descended on her, insistently pressing her down. His hard, lean body dug into her, twisting and pushing, mindless and cruel, determined only to have its own way. "You animal!" she spat out. "I loathe you!" The words only drove him to even more savage onslaughts. Nick surged into the beckoning red target, his muscles brutally thrusting and ramming, his arms tightening around like a vise.

"You animal!" This time it was a moan half of pleasure as she dug her nails into his back, and she began to stir beneath him. His drive intensified, and her own tempo accelerated now, her body moving in long, pulsing rhythms of inexpressible pleasure. She moaned and whimpered, twisted and shivered as a thrill of astonished ecstasy shuddered through her body. "Oh, beautiful!" she gasped. "I didn't know it could be like this!" And he knew that this time she wasn't acting, that she meant it. But there was no time now to wonder how that could be.

As he approached shuddering fulfillment, he felt her body arch incredibly, stiffen and hold. Her fingers tightened convulsively, dug into his flesh. The pupils of her eyes dilated and she screamed, "What's happening to me?" Then both their bodies were mindlessly welded together in one long, wonderfully savage moment of sublime, deep satisfaction.

They rested for a moment, drawing breath.

The moment of peace, however, was mercilessly brief. Nick's mind was racing. What had just happened to her never had before. And yet, the last time . . . He turned toward her. How could she be so incredibly different in her reactions each time?

It was time to find out. He kissed her. Her eyes opened. From her pupils, and from the way she had trouble focusing them, he knew that Editing's truth serum had begun to take effect.

"Darling, let's talk," he whispered.

"Yes . . . talk. . . ." she murmured vaguely.

Nick knew he didn't have much time. He proceeded directly to the heart of the matter—Juan Ochoa, alias Pedro Villareal, and the hit-and-run "accident."

"Were you present when your fiancée was killed?" he demanded with sudden harshness. She shuddered slightly, either at his tone or at what he'd said, and shook her head. "That's odd," he said in a voice as cold as an arctic wind, and went on to tell her in savage detail about the blonde in the white convertible who'd been seen driving away, and of the dented fender of her own car.

Her eyes flew open, struggling to focus. "You're not trying to say . . . but I loved Pedro. . . ."

"You'd better tell me about it," he snapped. "*All* about it."

And she did. "He was staying here . . . at the hotel . . . we met . . . accidentally, I thought . . . we saw a lot of each other . . . I grew fond of him . . . then, there was something he said one day . . . I knew then that our meeting hadn't been accidental, that he had planned it . . . there was a violent argument . . . on the beach here at the Sea-Top. . . ."

"What about?" Nick interrupted. "Be specific."

". . . I felt that he didn't really love me . . . that he was spying on me . . . it seemed to me he was placing my father in grave danger . . . I stormed away, determined never to see him again. . . . Later, I thought better of it . . . I thought perhaps he could help me . . . thought he might even be a government agent of some type . . . I phoned him . . ."

"From your father's house?"

"Yes . . . told him I'd meet him on the causeway . . . it seemed a good place . . . we wouldn't be overheard there . . . but . . ." She rubbed her forehead, as if straining to remember. ". . . don't know what happened . . . I never went . . . I seemed to collapse . . . When I came to, Dr. Orff told me that Pedro had been killed by a hit-and-run driver and that when he had first told me of it I had collapsed . . . "

"What is it that you were going to tell Pedro?" Nick demanded. "Was it something about Orff and your father? About the Cape Sable project?"

She nodded and started to reply—but Nick interrupted her. "Wait a minute!" he said tensely—for he suddenly felt the old familiar skin-tightening sensation of danger creeping up the back of his neck. "Was it Orff who sent you here tonight?"

Again she nodded, and smiled dreamily. She stretched herself luxuriously, murmuring, "To seduce you, darling . . . so glad I took his advice . . . put on my sexiest underthings . . . my slinkiest dress . . . didn't want to bring that silly handbag, though . . . he insisted. . . ."

The hair stood straight out on the back of Nick's neck.

The handbag!

All evening something had been pounding at his brain for attention. That was it! From the corner of his eye he saw it—on a chair to the left of the bed. His first instinct was to leap toward it, throw it the length of the room. An even stronger instinct told him not to, that there wasn't time. He gave Ingra a violent shove that sent her spinning off the opposite end of the bed. He followed, landing on top of her.

At the same instant, there was a blinding flash of light. The walls of the room seemed to expand outward. There was a roar as if the whole world were exploding, and then blackness swept over them. . . .

Chapter 11

A SOUTHERN BELLE STRUTS
HER STUFF

Julie had been staring into the barrel of the gun so long she was almost hypnotized by it. Ten minutes? Two hours? She'd lost track of time. It was a stalemate. Dunlap was unwilling to shoot her, yet he kept saying, "If you leave this office alive I'll be ruined."

He claimed he'd come back to get some papers he'd forgotten, had seen the door open and had entered with drawn gun. "Do all psychiatrists pack snub-nosed .38s?" Julie had asked, crossing her elegant legs and lighting a cigarette nonchalantly.

"All right, so I knew you were here!" he snapped. "I leave little traps around for snoopers and you fell into one. Why are you so interested in Ingra Brand, anyway? Who do you work for?"

"More to the point, who do *you* work for?" Julie had asked sweetly.

But the ensuing discussion had convinced her that Dunlap was no foreign agent, simply someone who'd allowed his integrity to be compromised by a sudden mad infatuation for a girl half his age. Nothing very earth-shaking about that—unless both parties happened to be employed on a top-secret government project. Then a nation's security became involved.

"But I tell you the girl is fantasizing," Dunlap had insisted. "That story about her father—it's such an obviously concocted cloak-and-dagger yarn. It would have ruined her career had it gotten into her record."

"Dr. Dunlap, to put it as charitably as I can," said

Julie, "your professional judgment has been clouded by your infatuation for the girl."

But Dunlap wasn't listening. "On these secret projects they expect everyone to be an automaton," he muttered angrily. "But brilliant people are often unstable."

Julie watched him closely. He was talking about himself as much as Ingra. She had an idea. "I think we can strike a bargain of sorts," she said carefully. "If you cooperate with me, I'll hold off mentioning your part in this as long as I can."

"Cooperate? How?"

"I want to see every note you've made on Ingra Brand's present psychic state. Do you still have them?"

He nodded. "They're in my quarters."

"Is it a deal, then?" she asked, holding out her hand for the gun. He thought about it for a while, then nodded, handing the gun to her with a sigh of relief. He buried his face in his hands, saying: "It's only a temporary condition." Then he suddenly glanced up—as if an idea had just struck him. "You'll be able to judge for yourself when she arrives back here. I'll arrange that you sit in on the reorientation session. Then, if you're still not convinced that she's cured, I'll go to Security myself and tell them about my part in this. Is *that* a deal?"

"*If* she comes back," said Julie.

"But that's just it," said Dunlap. "Security passed the wire on to me earlier this evening. She's returning to Cape Sable the first thing tomorrow morning."

Ingra Brand was screaming at the top of her lungs.

"Pappi! Ilse!" she shrieked, eyes bulging with horror, blood oozing from the corner of her mouth. "In the bunker . . . help me, someone . . . my sister and father . . . help. . . ."

Nick knelt beside her in the flaming wreckage of the room, checking the cuts and bruises they had both suffered. Fortunately all minor. The blood they were spitting up came from the impact of the explosion against their eardrums. As he staggered to his feet he saw that it was the big triple-decker sandwich of a bed that had saved them. Lucky thing it was flush with the floor. Otherwise their bodies would now be torn into as many fragments as the smoking mattress.

Cyclonite or RDX, figured Nick, molded into the lining of the purse and triggered by a timing device. Shaped in such a way as to explode horizontally—for they were supposed to have been on the beach with the purse right beside them. The valuable diamond was to have guaranteed that; Nick telling Ingra not to tempt fate by wearing it, but to put it in her handbag, and she keeping it right beside her for safety.

So they had meant to kill Ingra as well as him!

There were shouts and screams and the sound of people running in the hall outside. The danger wasn't over. Orff and company were sure to have observers spotted here and there to report back the results. They would strike again.

Nick glanced around. He had to get Ingra out of here and aboard the *Mobile Gal*. That was the only safe place now. Her clothes, which had been on the chair beside the purse, were totally destroyed. His shirt would do, though. He pulled it around her limp, unprotesting torso and buttoned it. It came almost to her knees. Then he pulled a pair of cotton shorts over his own nakedness, and guided her through the smoke and flames to the door. The hallway was crammed full of panic-stricken hotel guests milling about in their nightclothes, trying to push aboard the elevators. Nick moved quickly through their midst, shielding Ingra as best he could from their shoving and elbowing, and headed down the stairs.

He stopped beneath a naked light bulb on the second landing and held Ingra's face up toward it. Her pupils were still distended, the expression vacant, sightless. The shock of the explosion coming on top of Editing's truth serum had apparently jarred her mind back to some childhood experience. Her mother's death in an air raid? No, she kept saying her sister! Once in English, once in German. Quite distinctly. *Schwesterlein*—little sister. Nick took her by the shoulders and shook her, then slapped her face. But it was useless. She was in deep shock. She stared at him blankly, then began whimpering. Something about pain, a river of fire, and then, once again, "Pappi! Ilse!"

He heaved her over his shoulder in the classic fireman's lift and continued on down the stairs. He descended all the way to the basement, then cut across the parking lot and through the deserted grounds toward the marina. It was also deserted. The night attendant was gone from his post—distracted, Nick supposed, by the explosion and the people running toward it. All the better.

It was time to see Professor Brand again. The answer to a lot of things lay with the professor, including what it was exactly that Ingra was raving about. He glanced sideways at her in the binnacle light as he swung the *Mobile Gal* out from the dock. She was leaning against the control panel, staring blankly ahead.

He would have to get her into the bunk below and, to make sure she stayed there while he went ashore, place her in a state of *sakti*—the "white sleep of innermost being." Nick had learned this yoga exercise from the Tashi Lama of Lhasa. Instantaneous sleep, unconsciousness, even complete anesthetization of the senses—all induced by finger pressure on the eyes and the back of the neck. Now Western science had achieved the same results with an electric current of 0.05 milliamperes pulsing steadily into the same physical regions. But Nick still preferred the old Tibetan way. It needed less equipment; one had to carry one's fingertips around anyway.

Nick cut the engine as soon as he was out of the crowded main channel, carried Ingra below and placed her in the spare bunk. She dropped off to sleep instantly under his skilled touch. He clambered topside again, relieved to know she would now remain peacefully unconscious through any amount of noise and shock. And there would be plenty of that, he realized as he glanced over his shoulder, hastily gunning the powerful twin diesels.

He saw the tiny spouts rise on the calm surface but couldn't hear the shots. They were still too far away—three or four miles at least. The dark, indistinct shape of the speedboat detached itself from the mainland and grew larger. More spouts rose in the water, closer this time.

Nick deliberated. There was a full moon and the tide was running with him. He saw the heavy slant seaward of the buoy he passed, with the current swirling at its base. Nick decided his best bet was to let his pursuers catch up, then give them a blast of the twin Bofers. By then they would both be beyond the reef and out of sight of land.

The reef showed almost abeam to starboard as the first bullets reached him. They went whanging off the side of the cockpit, churning up the water ahead. Nick fitted the special key into the control panel and pressed the fourth button over. That would bring the 40mm Bofers sliding out of what looked like twin exhaust pipes. He glanced over his shoulder. The speedboat was practically on top of him now. It was a sleek, powerful Owens XL 19. There was a man on the flying bridge, a submachine gun bulky in his hands. Two men were aft, rifles held to their shoulders, firing. As they roared across his wake, Nick pressed the fifth button over. The red one.

The *Mobile Gal* shook beneath the powerful cannon thrusts. Nick held the button down as the tracers zipped into the speedboat in great red stitches, making a hiccoughing *bof bof bof* noise. The Owens shuddered beneath the impact like a living thing. It literally dissolved into flaming fragments before his eyes. He saw the figures billowing up through the orange inferno like rag dolls. Hot air blasted into his face. He swung away, bringing his own vessel hard about.

As he did, he sighted the two hydrofoils. They came roaring around No Name Key and under the causeway, skimming over the dark surface of the water toward him like giant grasshoppers. They were doing at least 80 knots. The muzzle flashes reached him before the roar did. Then suddenly the slugs were making the sound of frightened pigeons whistling overhead. Nick reacted with the speed of a striking snake, cutting the diesels, flicking the key, pressing the button that said *J46 Start*. There wasn't a second to spare. The *Mobile Gal* had to show herself for what she was—and fast!

A low, hollow rumble came from amidships. A light blinked on the panel to show that the turbojet was firing properly. Nick flicked two more switches, activating the stabilizer fins. At the same time, he pressed the buttons that brought the forward deck back and the .50-caliber Browning quads up and into position.

One of the hydrofoils came hurtling across his bow, its forward machine gun blazing. Nick pressed the red button. His quads hammered back. He saw the glass of the hydrofoil's cockpit bridge shatter, a figure spin away from the heavy m.g. he'd been manning. The hydrofoil went careening off on its metal skids like a woman in high heels surprised by a mouse, her skirts held high.

Nick seized the opportunity to get under way. He glanced over his shoulder at the blue-green flame of the afterburner, quickly pulled the electromagnetic gear shift to *Slow Ahead,* and the cruiser began to move.

The hydrofoils came skidding around on either side of her. They had already sized up the situation, knew they didn't have a second to lose. A radio-controlled 57mm recoilless rifle suddenly opened up on the one to port. It hit short, and seawater geysered over the *Mobile Gal's* afterdeck. They were trying to knock out the turbojet!

Nick slammed the gear shift to *Full Ahead.* The cruiser trembled, settled to stern briefly, then surged forward. Fast. Faster. Nick watched the dials, his hand on the lever at his side. At 5000 h.p., *Gal* lifted out of the water, half flying, half planing across the glittering sheet of moonlit water.

Tracers tore through the night, converging on her from both sides, tearing long splinters in the deck, slamming into the superstructure. Nick glanced over his shoulder. Through the shuddering green flame of the afterburner he saw the hydrofoils slowly receding, their fire beginning to fall short. He aimed his flying steel bullet straight for the channel under the causeway. The speedometer inched forward—99, 100, and still he didn't have her full out. "God bless you, Frankie Gennaro, and all your descendants," breathed Nick fervently.

But outdistancing the hydrofoils wouldn't be enough, he knew. They were aware of the secret cove on the windward side of No Name and would simply wait for him to emerge from it later. He had to destroy them. Now.

As he shot out the far side of the causeway, Nick glanced back, saw the hydrofoils converging on the channel. Although they drew only four feet of water, they apparently didn't want to chance the other approaches. This was the place to do it, then. His fist hit the lever marked "P."

A drag parachute billowed open, slowing the *Mobile Gal* with such suddenness that Nick felt his stomach squeeze up into his throat. He hit the switch that cut the parachute loose, then punched the last button on the control panel and swung around in his stool. The fishing seats flipped over and a succession of small canisters began rolling down special chutes, plopping into the cruiser's wake. He saw them strung out behind for a couple of hundred yards, bobbing brightly in the moonlight.

When the hydrofoils reached the first of them, a flash of searing white light exploded across the darkness, illuminating everything for miles around as if it were daylight. There was no sound except for the hydrofoils' engines and Nick's own diminishing turbojet. Then there were two smaller, orange explosions, followed by twin claps of thunder, and suddenly men and equipment were tumbling through the eerie sheet of silent white flame. The aluminum skids on the hydrofoils melted, curling up under the blazing wreckage like an insect's tendrils. Then the flame diminished, and Nick saw cars halting along the causeway and people leaping from them, pointing and gesturing excitedly.

Minutes later, the *Mobile Gal* arrived at the cove. She came in fast, then slowly lowered herself into the water as the turbojet cut off. Her arrival brought small waves that lapped and sucked at the beach and then were still. The figure who swam ashore didn't pause at the boathouse to change disguises or personalities. He simply emptied shoes, a shirt, pants, Luger and a small pellet from the waterproof bag, quickly dressed and distributed the armaments about his person, then moved on silent cat feet up the slope and along the deserted track toward Senior City.

Beneath the royal palms, the inky darkness folded in around the few street lamps like a cloak. Nick made no attempt to conceal himself. It would have been a waste of time after the spectacular naval battle. Besides, that afternoon's experience in Senior City had convinced him that all the usual precautions were a waste of time.

CLAW did not bother with such minor details as sentries and lookouts. They didn't have to. They were fully automated.

Nick waved and mugged it up for the closed-circuit monitor which he felt certain was filming his approach along K Street.

Chapter 12

Direct frontal assault—that was how N3 had planned it. He moved cautiously through the thick, viscous shadows of K Street, the gas pellet called Pierre nestled in his right hand.

The houses which lined both sides of the quiet residential street were lit up like Christmas trees. Lights blazed in every room. But Nick saw no people in any of them, heard no voices, nor any of the usual, everyday sounds of living. Were they just props—like everything else in Senior City?

Where were all the oldsters he'd seen around that afternoon? Nick had a pretty good idea—doubling back past him to reach the *Mobile Gal*. Let them, he thought grimly. Ingra was not on board. He'd left her concealed on a reef just outside the cove. What *was* on board, waiting for them, was death. In the form of a 25-pound charge of RDX, triggered to go off if one climbed aboard the cruiser without first reaching up and cutting the concealed electric circuit.

Professor Brand's house was the only one on the block that was dark. As Nick approached it, he saw shadowy figures dart across the lawn. A car immediately pulled away from the curb and accelerated down the street. Rats deserting the ship? Or just part of the trap?

Through the half-raised blinds Nick could see Professor Brand sitting in his wheelchair in the living room. The flickering, bluish light of a TV set illuminated the old man and the book-lined walls. The monitor on which his approach was being recorded? N3 worked his way through the shadows toward the side window. No, a regular program apparently, a panel show of some type. Strange, he wouldn't have thought the professor. . . . Suddenly he felt the back of his neck creep.

Judas!

The image on the TV set had only lasted a split second, but there was no mistaking the stiff, square shoulders, the bullet head fronted by that flat, expressionless face that looked as if it had been carelessly stitched on. Now the TV was blank, a blue-gray eye staring into the darkened room. Some panel show! thought Nick as he moved back into the shadows and headed toward the rear of the house. "The Brain Wash Hour! Brought to you by CLAW, manufacturers of hatred, murder and the seeds of war, with hundreds of handy, convenient branch offices the world over."

And this, he was sure, was one of them. Nick tested a drainpipe for strength, then started up it with his feet braced against the stucco wall, his strong hands drawing him upward. At the top, he stretched his flexible, yoga-trained body toward the window he'd spotted on the right.

Something about it bothered him. Hugo flicked out of his wrist sheath and probed beneath the sash, lifting it slightly while he hugged the wall to one side. Pffft! The sound was like that of a cobra striking. Nick glanced across at the next house to see the dart embedded in the blank wall, its delicate shaft still quivering. Cautiously, he raised the window the rest of the way and swung himself into the room. The crossbow had been rigged so as to discharge the dart when the window was raised. Some welcome!

He crept silently through the upper rooms but found nothing. Then he started down the heavily carpeted stairs. The professor was still watching TV, his back to Nick, sitting hunched forward in the wheelchair. There was no sound but a faint buzzing from the set. When N3 moved further into the room he saw why—the split image on the screen was of the empty, deserted street outside. Both directions! He'd guessed right.

Nick's thoughts leaped ahead with computerlike speed,

reeling through a cause-and-effect pattern which hadn't as yet happened. The result was that Hugo was in his hand and he was swinging on the balls of his feet before he even felt the warning buzzer go off in his brain.

The squat, blunt-faced Cuban in the white *guayabera* was caught short. He was still in the hallway behind Nick, drawing the heavy, axlike machete from the decorative wall scabbard in which it hung. Nick was on him in one stride. Hugo slid into the Cuban's heart from the rear. His hands and legs splayed away from the scabbard. His face strained back toward Killmaster, and there seemed to be almost relief in the bulging eyes before the whites rolled upward. Then a strangled noise came from the open mouth and the squat, ugly body crashed to the floor.

"Professor Brand," said Nick, swinging toward him. "Are you. . . ." The words froze in his mouth. So he'd finally made it, the fatal mistake that expunges an agent's name from the active rolls and places it instead on a bronze plaque of honor back at headquarters. The K.I.A. plaque—Killed in Action. N3 boiled with rage and frustration. It had been so obvious, yet he'd overlooked it—the possibility that Brand had been play-acting that afternoon, that he was actually on CLAW's side. It should have registered when he'd seen Brand watching the monitor, but the image of Judas had caused him to jump to the wrong conclusion—that Brand was being brainwashed rather than receiving instructions.

Nick stared at the cane which Professor Brand was pointing at him. It was a rifle with a skeleton butt which was also a twist breech. The squat bulge of a silencer had taken the place of the rubber tip.

"Barrel from the Remington 721," said Brand, smiling "Takes the .300 Magnum cartridge. Two of them."

"Excellent for elephants." Nick smiled back.

"Into the corner!" snapped Brand. "Face the wall."

Strange, thought Nick. This was not the same voice Brand had had that afternoon. N3 was an expert on voices. In learning how to imitate them, he'd come to know every nuance of tone, could classify them into eight basic types, could even link the changes and combinations that were possible. The change from this afternoon to now was not one of them.

"If you kill me, or even detain me," said Nick casually "you'll be destroying your own daughter."

He watched Brand from the corner of his eye. No reaction. Brand was busy pulling a pair of handcuffs from beneath the blanket that covered his legs. "Put your hands behind your back," he ordered, wheeling toward him.

N3's leg shot out, the metal heel of his shoe catching beneath the wheelchair's footrest. He heaved upward with all his might. The cane thudded heavily and plaster came pouring down on both of them. Nick whirled around as the chair tipped over with a crash. Its occupant was no cripple. He spun to the right, jackknifing to one knee, the cane pointed at Nick. Nick ducked as the cane thudded again, and felt the bullet whistle past his ear and slam into the wall behind him.

"That's your second and last, friend," he said, his eyes cold and hard. The fist with the long steel finger, and all of Nick's arm and shoulder behind it, lunged into the man's neck at approximately the point the mask began. Blood welled up behind the Lastotex like mercury in a thermometer, blotting out the features. The man sank to the floor.

N3 pulled the blood-soaked mask away and stared grimly at the "senior citizen" who lay revealed. Layer upon layer of deception, thought Nick disgustedly. Beneath this face would be another bloody mask—but of flesh and blood. Surgery prevented his going any further. Wheels within wheels, stroke and counter-stroke, twist upon complicated twist, and all leading—where?

Nick pulled the blinds, locked the doors and windows and searched the house from top to bottom. There was no sign of the real Professor Brand, nor of Dr. Orff. Nor of anyone else, for that matter. They had vanished into the night. Those running figures? The car pulling away? They must have seen his approach on the monitor and fled, leaving behind enough traps to slow him down, if not kill him.

Nick checked the TV set carefully. It was a standard make, and the other channels were legitimate. Key West,

Miami and Fort Myers stations came in on them. The channel containing the closed circuit image of the street was a UHF one, but no amount of fiddling with the controls would bring back Judas' image.

Nick found the two cameras in a room on the second floor, filming the street through the venetian blinds. There was a second monitor in this room, also on. It showed a split image of the approach from the beach through the backyard and the house and driveway directly across the street. There was a chair in front of the set and a cigarette still burning in an ashtray on the floor. Nick picked it up and sniffed it. Cuban brand. So his squat friend in the *guayabera* had been a recent arrival!

A locked closet beneath the stairs gave way to Nick's Lockpicker's Special and revealed a miniature darkroom equipped with sink and faucet as well as 35mm cameras, film, developers, photographic papers, equipment for making microdots, and a high-powered microscope. A cabinet over the sink contained a miniature radio transmitter and a transistorized RDF able to translate a signal from a radio beacon into a line direction, and then express that line in degrees.

Nick wondered what beacon it was tuned to. He switched it on and made his "fix," then checked it against the chart of Big Pine Key and its environs tacked to the wall above the transmitter. At first he couldn't make sense of it. The beacon was right here on K Street. Then, as he moved back from the apparatus, he saw the needle on a dial fall from 100 to 90. He stepped forward again. It jumped back to 100. *He was the beacon!*

In a flash, the events of that afternoon became clear. *That* was how those "senior citizens" had been able to track him to the boathouse! And *that* was undoubtedly why the chase hadn't begun until after he'd left Brand's house. A routine check of the RDF had alerted them to who he really was. Beautiful! thought Nick savagely. There was still enough XL fluid in his bloodstream to make him a walking target! Nothing he could do about it now, though. Nick willed his mind back to the task at hand—the search.

A second cabinet contained a box filled with makeup and masks, all of them incredibly lifelike. One or two of them looked vaguely like certain citizens of Big Pine, but it was impossible to tell exactly who they were supposed to represent without first fitting them onto a living face. Nick took the waterproof bag from his pocket and unfolded it. He placed a sample of everything he'd found in the closet in it, and then locked the door and went into Professor Brand's ground-floor bedroom. There were personal letters in a bureau drawer. Nick flipped through them. Most were from fellow scientists, requesting information and advice. A few, however, were from Ingra Brand, postmarked "Flamingo, Florida"—Cape Sable's cover address. These Nick stuffed into the bag.

His fingers now reached deep into the drawer and upward to stroke the underside of the bureau top. A small piece of paper was taped to it. He worked it loose. The paper came out in one piece. Scribbled across it was the combination to a safe.

Nick straightened up, glancing around the room. The safe would doubtless be behind a picture. But there were none. Then behind furniture. He pulled the bed out, then the bureau—and there it was. Brand had certainly not taken any great precautions to hide the safe. Nick squatted down, his glove-covered fingers working at the combination lock.

A bundle of papers came out in Nick's groping hand, then a large manila envelope stuffed with pictures. N3 hastily leafed through them. They were faded, dog-eared snapshots full of swastikas and jackboots. Some were of scientific groups posing before mock-ups of submarines and other secret weapons; others of scuba-geared frogmen lined up for inspection; one of Brand himself standing beside a tall, wolf-faced man—Admiral Canaris of the Abwehr. There were some of civilians and military around large conference tables staring stonily into the camera; still others of family groups; a couple of Brand and his fellow scientists being greeted by the Führer himself.

Nick leafed through the papers. Most were letters, in German, with dates ranging from 1939 to 1946. He stuffed them into the waterproof bag, closed the safe and switched off the downstairs monitor. He did the same upstairs, then let himself out the same window by which he had entered, slid down the drainpipe, and moved off into the shadows.

Nick was mildly surprised to find the *Mobile Gal* intact. He'd purposely circled back via the shoreline, scouting for a possible replacement. He had come across a 21-foot Chris-Craft runabout moored to a private jetty and had made a mental note to return for it should he find his own cabin cruiser blown to smithereens. But it wasn't. It swayed gently at its moorings in the quiet, moonlit cove, obviously untouched.

After gingerly disconnecting the RDX charge, Nick swung himself aboard her and cast off. Minutes later he arrived off the point where Bonefish Shoal broke the surface. He slid the *Mobile Gal* to within a cable's length of the hunk of dead coral, then waded in the rest of the way on foot. Ingra lay as he had left her, cushioned by sea grape, a tarpaulin spread over her, breathing deeply and regularly.

Nick stood there a moment, gazing down at her in the moonlight. Her head was turned toward him and, as he looked, a quick breath of wind pulled a length of blonde hair across her face, whipping long strands over her cheek, lacing itself across her eyes like a silken veil. At that moment Ingra resembled nothing so much as Botticelli's Venus, risen from the sea. He bent down, pulled back the tarpaulin and gently gathered her into his arms. *Knock it off,* he told himself savagely. He still had no proof that she hadn't killed Ochoa, that she wasn't actually an enemy agent.

He carried her out to the cabin cruiser, placed her on the afterdeck, then swung himself aboard. For all he knew, this might not even be her own face. N3 was so mask-happy by now that he actually parted her hair with his fingers, searching for any telltale surgery scars. There were none. Her face was her own.

But who was she?

Five hours later that question was the most important Nick Carter had ever asked himself.

He had spent the night anchored off Bonefish Shoal, sitting in the control cockpit, eyes and ears peeled for the enemy while plans had spun through his agile mind like an unreeling film.

Now, at dawn, he was ready to communicate with AXE headquarters, to file a complete report on every aspect of the case to date, and to let them know where he was headed, what his next moves would be. This way, if anything went wrong, his replacement would not be sent in cold.

It was too early for Hawk himself to be at his desk, and Ray Johnson of Communications was taping Nick's report when he suddenly interrupted him with news 50 times more startling than any Nick had for AXE.

"This just came in," said Johnson in his deceptively laconic Tennessee drawl, and he read it directly off the transcript to Nick:

"TRANSMISSION 8096-J. 5:46 AM. AGENT JULIA BARON REPORTS INGRA BRAND HAS JUST RETURNED CAPE SABLE PROJECT."

N3's face was usually impassive. Never did it betray an emotion he didn't wish it to. But this time he couldn't control it, didn't even try to. He just gaped—first at the shortwave radio set, then at the girl in the bunk.

If Ingra Brand was at Cape Sable, then who in hell was this?

Chapter 13

The girl in the bunk stirred. Her eyes flew open. She looked at the tall, steely-eyed man with the slightly unruly dark hair who was bending over her, and snatched at the sheet, pulling it up around her neck. *"Wie heissen Sie?"* she gasped.

The outspread fingers of Nick Carter's right hand moved from the girl's temples down to her throat and closed around it—but lightly. They rested there, his thumb barely touching the throbbing carotid artery. Very casually, lighting a cigarette with his other hand, N3 said, "Who exactly are you, sweetheart?"

The blank eyes filled with tears. The little girl's voice whispered:*"Mein name ist Ingra. Ich habe mich verlaufen. Sind hier Amerikanische soldaten in der Nahe?"* It was useless, Nick saw. She was still deep in shock, reliving some childhood experience of war. "My name is Ingra," she had said. "I'm lost. Are there American soldiers around here?" Pointless to put her through it: He massaged her temples, pressing his thumbs against her eyeballs, and she dropped off to sleep once again.

Nick climbed into the control cockpit and had a look around. The sun was still low on the horizon, its reflection blindingly brilliant on the mirrorlike surface of Florida Bay. He glanced at his watch. 6:15 A.M. At AXE headquarters Condition Red Alert had been declared. Hawk was already on his way in, being briefed by radiophone as his chauffeured limousine swept through Washington traffic. He would contact N3 as soon as he could learn more details about Julie Baron's report. Until then, there was nothing more that could be done.

Nick flicked on the ignition. The *Mobile Gal*'s twin diesels rumbled to life. Time to get going. Peligro Key was a good 20 miles away. Peligro. Spanish for danger, he thought grimly. Danger Key. Well named. Everything pointed to it as the nerve center of CLAW's activities. The televised image he had seen of Judas meant that he was probably within 30 miles of Big Pine. Closed circuits didn't operate much beyond that. And the mysterious A.K. Atchinson and his equally mysterious Aquacity— they both smelled to high heaven, in N3's opinion. Nobody, not even an eccentric Texas oil millionaire, would bother defending a purely commercial project with a rifle-toting army. And then there was the disappearance of Brand and Orff. Nick was sure they had also gone to Peligro.

Brand. A big question mark. Nick had spent the predawn hours poring over the photographs and papers he'd found in Brand's safe, wondering if he were really the victim of brainwashing, as he had at first seemed. Those blueprints he'd drawn up for an underwater invasion of England. What would they be doing in his safe 25 years after the non-event? Surely they were only of historical interest now? *Or had they actually been drawn up so long ago?* Despite the dates and geographical references, much of the equipment looked strangely modern. The underwater sleds and tractors, the two-man wet subs, all incorporated principles and parts that hadn't been developed in 1941.

The Contents Keys stretched toward Peligro like coral footsteps. Then came a big jump—four miles of open water. But Nick didn't make that jump. For the next two hours he cautiously maneuvered the *Mobile Gal* among the Contents Keys, traveling at snail's pace, the diesels turning over as quietly as he could run them, the exhaust bubbling glutinously, a thread of blue vapor rising astern.

The Keys were a perfect baffle against radar, but Nick would have liked to get in closer. Four miles was one helluva long underwater swim. He had no choice, though. The next to last island in the group, Shark Key, looked like the perfect spot in which to leave both gals—the *Mobile* and the one who called herself Ingra. A small L-shaped cove at its south end was ringed by trees high enough to conceal the cabin cruiser from prying eyes.

An incoming signal on the shortwave set buzzed as Nick was making the vessel secure in her moorings.

It was Hawk. "Julie Baron's report has now been fully confirmed," his voice crackled. "Ingra Brand returned to the NASA base at Cape Sable at 5:45 this morning. Julie advised Major Bessler of NASA Security and Dr. Dunlap, the project psychologist, of your information and, under medical pretexts, the girl representing herself as Ingra Brand was given a thorough physical examination. After that, she was given an extensive security check and Julie herself sat in—unobserved, of course—on the reorientation session. At its conclusion all three parties—Major Bessler, Dunlap and Julie—report that they are thoroughly convinced that the girl really is Ingra Brand."

N3 glanced over his shoulder at the blonde sleeping in his bunk. Then he said a surprising thing. He said: "I think they both are."

Hawk's voice was chipped ice. "Would you mind clarifying that statement?" he snapped.

Nick's trained mind was racing now, assembling a line from a letter here, a photograph there, challenging each new piece of evidence, then accepting it when no objections could be found to it. Slowly a picture began to emerge. N3 said: "I need a few minutes. Please stand by. I'll recontact you." He immediately began flipping through the photos he'd taken from Brand's safe—a safe, he realized now, that was meant to keep things not from Orff and Company, but from his daughter. The photo—where was it? It was the key to everything. His fingers closed around it eagerly, held it up, turned it over. Scribbled on the back was the notation, "Berchtesgaden, Juli, 1943."

It was a photo of Hitler's assembled brain trust and their wives and children, full of *gemutlichkeit* and beer on a sun-soaked balcony, the snow-capped Alps in the background. Nick's finger picked out Professor Brand, standing slightly apart from the others. He looked withdrawn, morose, and the black armband he wore explained why. He had just lost his wife in an air raid. The three-year-old blonde girl standing beside him, however, was beaming and happy, without a care in the world. But was she really standing beside *him?* At first glance, Nick had thought so. But now, a second, careful look established that she actually was closer to the next family over—by a good six inches at least.

Six inches that made all the difference!

The woman, blonde, pretty in a beefy kind of way, bore a striking resemblance to the little girl. And the man —those shining glasses, the steel-wool hair! N3 knew him —Professor Lautenbach! And next to him, her face half buried in his trouser leg, peeking out, laughing—another blonde moppet, *an exact replica of the first!*

Twins! Professor Lautenbach's twin daughters!

Lautenbach, Hitler's evil scientific genius who didn't die in the Führer's Berlin bunker as everyone had thought, but who later turned up working for Judas and CLAW in Red China! N3 had last seen him in the control booth of a secret missile base in Outer Mongolia, only seconds before the explosion Nick had engineered had blown Lautenbach and his deadly handiwork to smithereens.

With computerlike speed, Nick's mind now assembled fragments of Ingra's ravings, guarded clues in Professor Brand's letters, snippets of information from other documents. What he got was: A direct hit on the bunker, Ingra thrown clear, the bunker bursting into flames, her father and twin sister caught inside. Only there was another exit that she didn't know about, a secret one perhaps, linking it with other bunkers—the Führer's, or, more likely, Martin Bormann's.

Ingra, meanwhile, went running through the flaming streets, crying for help. And then? At some later point Brand had adopted Ingra, Nick figured. He had raised her as his own, never telling her the truth. Keeping what he'd done secret would have been no problem in 1945, when practically every record in Germany had been destroyed. And Ingra's twin sister? She hadn't died in that Berlin bunker any more than her father had. Instead, she had accompanied him to Red China where—

graced with Western looks and her father's ruthless, amoral brilliance—she had become a top CLAW operative!

"It makes sense," Hawk admitted at the conclusion of Nick's report. "A great deal of sense. Good thinking, son. It tallies with a number of the things that Julie has uncovered at her end." And he briefly reviewed the information that she had dredged from Dunlap's files, describing him pointedly as "the project's *ex*-psychologist."

Then, after a dramatic pause, Hawks' voice suddenly crackled over the airwaves: "There's only one problem, however. Which is which? Everything points to the fact that *your* Ingra is the real one, of course, but until we know exactly what CLAW is up to we can't be sure. I've just finished making arrangements with Major Bessler that will give Julie free run of the entire project, and I've ordered her to stick like a burr to her Ingra."

"Things are definitely coming to a head at this end," said Nick, and he gave Hawk a quick rundown on his projected underwater exploration of Peligro.

The old man was silent for a moment. Then the words came crackling in over the scrambler, and Nick scowled at hearing them. "A replacement?" he repeated. "But why on earth, at this point?"

"I spoke to the doctors in Miami," said Hawk, "and they take full responsibility over this XL fluid business, but they also made a valid point. Very little is known as yet about the substance. Their tests showed that they had removed it all from your bloodstream. Your own report indicates that faint traces of it remain. They can make no prediction about how much longer it will take to work its way out. Meanwhile, you're placing yourself in grave and unnecessary danger."

"Is the decision up to me?" interrupted Nick. "Or is it out of my hands?" Hawk replied that it was up to him. "Then I want to continue," said N3.

Hawk's only comment was, "I wanted you to know there was an alternative." Then he added: "We've only got forty-eight hours. Whatever CLAW is planning, it's going to happen before then. Major Bessler told me that a test firing is planned for 10 A.M. Tuesday. The PHO missile, minus its warhead, will be shot down the Ascension Island range in an accuracy test. I'll expect a definitive report from you twenty-four hours prior to that."

Twenty-four hours! The old dynamo certainly demanded swift action, thought Nick as he signed off. It meant that whatever N3 might be doing 24 hours from now, he'd have to drop it and get on the radio to Hawk, or someone else would be on the way to take over—perhaps to look for whatever pieces of Nicholas J. Huntington Carter were still floating on the ocean's surface!

Nick made a final check of his gear. He patted the black wet suit he was wearing. Pierre was zipped into a waterproof side pocket. Hugo's pencil-like sheath was in place, just inside the rubber wrist lining. A second knife—large, blue-handled—was strapped to his leg. It was to fend off sharks as well as men. Wilhelmina was not going with him, however. The Luger would be useless underwater. He patted it sadly and said goodbye, placing it inside the Peebee box with the rest of his equipment and papers. He slid the special compartment shut, locked it, snapped the key onto the chain around his neck and shoved it inside the wet suit. Then, having taken a last look at the girl sleeping peacefully in the bunk, he climbed out onto the afterdeck.

The noonday sun blazed down, frying him inside the hot rubber suit. Nick leaned over, fitting the blue flippers onto his feet. Then he heaved the aqua-lung cylinders onto his back and adjusted the webbing at his waist. He fitted the rubber mouthpiece between his teeth and adjusted the valve release until the air supply was just right. Then he bent over the side, spat into his mask to prevent its steaming up, rinsed it out, adjusted it. He took a last look around and then swung over the side.

The coral shelved steeply and Nick kept going down until, at about 24 feet, he was only inches above the bottom. He untensed his muscles and put his legs into an easy, relaxed rhythm. He had a long swim ahead of him. It didn't pay to rush. As he emerged from the narrow confines of the cove, he pointed his body like a compass needle along the course he would follow to Peligro and set out, swimming in a giant, easy crawl. The light was soft and milky and the shadows of the surface waves curled across the sand below. Nick glanced over his shoulder, watching the telltale bubbles streaming up in a fountain of silver pearls. He hoped the small waves hid them. When he got in closer he would have to switch the air supply off and resort to yoga.

Nick swam steadily for an hour, ignoring the jeweled butterfly and angel fish that flirted with his mask, the anemones with their crimson centers that waved their velvet tentacles at him, the hairy sea centipedes that scurried out of his way. Once the great streamers of a Portuguese man-of-war floated past only inches above his head, and he ducked, knowing that if they caught a man across the heart they could kill him.

But his warning system was particularly attuned to those unexplained heavy movements and swirls in the water that meant man or shark was in the vicinity. Each time he felt one, he would whirl around, staring into the milky gloom. Once a barracuda came near, its angry tiger's eyes glaring at him from so close that Nick could see its gills working softly and the teeth glinting like a wolf's along its cruel underslung jaw. After carefully examining him, the great fish veered away into the gloom, and Nick continued on his way.

Peligro took him by surprise. He had expected to be forewarned of his approach to it by Aquacity which, according to the brochures, should have been spread out from south to east, directly across his path. But there was no Aquacity. And no signs that there ever had been or was to be such a place. No equipment, no activity on the ocean floor. Just sand and water. Then suddenly the coral shelf of the island itself hove into view, climbing steeply toward the surface.

Danger Key. He had reached it.

Nick took a last, gulping breath, then cut the air supply and kicked his way up through the misty gray water. A sharp pain needled into his ears. Nick jackknifed his body back down and hung there, paddling, about ten feet below the surface until he had decompressed enough for the pain to vanish. Then, cautiously, he floated back up, stopping as soon as his eyes broke water.

He made a complete turn, saw there were no boats in the vicinity, and concentrated on the island which lay approximately 800 yards away. A. K. Atchinson's villa overwhelmed everything else, rising on an artificial slope from the key's coral base, its verdant lawn dotted with stands of palmetto and citrus with a larger fringe of hardwoods and palms. Strung out along the waterline was a complex of jetties, warehouses and barges. Four hydrofoils were moored to one jetty, and a half-dozen men in aqua-lungs sat along its taffrail, their frogmen's feet dangling over the side. A large flatboat with a covered shade was moored nearby, the deck a tangle of ropes, aqua-lungs, wet rubber suits, blue-handled knives, sealed lights, rebreathers, flippers, CO_2 spear guns and lead weights. A man wearing a visored cap and a blue denim uniform stood leaning against the flatboat's stanchion, looking out to sea, a submachine gun hanging by a strap from his left shoulder.

As Nick's eyes moved slowly along the shoreline, he saw more gun-bearing figures, some with binoculars dangling from their necks. A number of gray and red underwater sleds equipped with spear-gun attachments and powered by electric motors were stacked on another jetty. N3 recognized them. He'd seen them in blueprint from among Professor Brand's papers. On a nearby cradle sat a fat, round, orange-and-black two-man submarine that had also been designed by Brand.

The other equipment that he saw was standard stuff —Westinghouse diving saucers, a Reynolds Aluminaut, a couple of Perry submarines, "mobots"—unmanned robot subs of a type used to tend underwater oil wells— an ocarina-shaped diving craft equipped with metal claws that could reach out and pick objects off the ocean floor. In a storage hangar a bit further on Nick sighted a group of men brushing fiberglass onto the struts of still another hydrofoil.

There was at least ten million dollars' worth of underwater equipment on the key, Nick realized as he submerged, swam a few hundred yards and rose once again to the surface—to find himself looking this time at a dock crowded with aluminum and glass tubing, much of it still in crates that were stenciled with the names of top U.S. manufacturing firms. All this equipment—*but no Aquacity!*

What did it mean?

To make doubly sure he hadn't missed the underwater project, Nick dived once again and circled Peligro completely. Nothing. Nothing but sand, water and natural coral formations to all sides of the key.

When he surfaced this time he had a close call. A hydrofoil came roaring toward him with men standing fore and aft, high-powered rifles cradled in their arms. N3 dived —in the nick of time. The great shadowy hull swept overhead and he was tumbled about like a rag doll by the turbulence of its huge, knifelike propellers. The hydrofoil didn't stop, however. He hadn't been sighted.

It was time to head back to Shark Key anyway, Nick decided as he checked his air supply. It would be dark soon and he didn't want Ingra to awake in panic and try to maneuver the boat out of the cove herself.

He made good time going back, concentrating only on keeping his face a few inches above the sand and his head well down to streamline his body. His relaxed, easy, distance-eating version of the Australian crawl brought Nick back to the underwater entrance of the cove in a little over an hour. He kicked upward, rising swiftly through his own silver air bubbles, and broke the surface.

The boat was gone. And so was Ingra.

Something heavy knocked against his shoulder. He reached around, pulled it toward him. It was a piece of wreckage, and he knew from its feel, construction and weight that it had been part of the *Mobile Gal*.

Chapter 14

Nowhere to go now but back—*to Danger Key*.

Nick checked his air supply. Enough for the last mile only. He would have to stick to the surface until then, hope that he wouldn't be sighted.

He set out with great overhand strokes, his body cutting through the dark water. The sun had set only moments before, but night had already closed in with tropical suddenness. In the darkness ahead, N3 could just make out the ocean's rim. Then came a layer of black haze above which the first stars winked.

Had they killed the girl? Taken her to Peligro? The *Mobile Gal* had not been rigged to explode this time. All Nick could figure was that they had blown her out of the water, probably with a recoilless rifle mounted on a hydrofoil. Probably hadn't even given warning, he thought grimly, so the chances of her having survived the attack were slim. Unless. . . .

Unless, of course, she had radioed them, directed them to where the vessel lay moored! How else, after all, had they been able to find the *Mobile Gal*?

This time it took him twice as long to cover the distance. The night trade wind was blowing, and the surface had grown rough. There was a heavy swell and deep troughs. A patch of phosphorus dripped jewels of light as Nick lifted one weary arm after the other from the water, cutting through it. When at last Peligro rose darkly from the horizon like a great ocean liner without running lights, Nick adjusted his face mask, put the mouthpiece between his teeth, turned on the air and dived.

There was a moon, but it was low on the horizon and did little good below. Nick glided through the murky darkness, shadowy forms of billfish and jack parting grudgingly before him. After awhile the rhythm of his steady progress became automatic, and the shapes of things became gradually more distinct. This time he didn't stop short of Peligro's coral slope, but climbed slowly up it, dragging water with his webbed gloves and thrusting with his feet, working smoothly but hard.

Nick's air supply was running out. It took him great, sucking breaths to get anything out of the tube at all. He glanced at the gauge. It was down into the fifth sector, with only seconds to go. That meant yoga from here on in, but that was all right. Judging from the pressure, he was only seconds from the surface. He took a last, long drag of air from the emptying cylinder, and held his breath.

He went clambering up over the sharp ridges of coral, his hand reaching out, fingers clawing for support. Suddenly his extrasensory antennae jangled—but too late. His hand had already closed around the wire. It snapped with a crackle of sparks, burning through the rubber, sending hot, searing pain piercing straight to his cerebellum. He rolled over, momentarily stunned and gasping for breath.

At the same instant, a heavy object plummeted into the water above Nick. He glanced up—in time to see a man in a black rubber suit come snaking down toward him. He held a CO_2 gun in his right hand and had extra quivers strapped to his leg. On his back was a compressed-air speed pack which propelled him downward with amazing speed.

Nick hurled himself toward him, flailing at the water with his fins. The man leveled the CO_2 gun. Nick saw that he would never make it. He was still four or five strokes from the man. He jackknifed himself downward, touching his toes as he balled himself into as small a target as possible. He felt the shock wave of the gas explosion against the small of his back, felt something glance off his shoulder. The bright needle of the spear went wavering slowly past him toward the depths. The man was pedaling furiously now as he thrust another spear down the barrel of the gun.

Nick snaked up toward him, his chest tight inside the rubber weave of the suit from the strain of holding his breath. Hugo was out of its sheath and in his hand now. It lunged toward the man, moving with terrifying slowness through the water. The blade went in. Nick could feel the black rubber against his hand, saw the man suddenly writhe and double up around the blade like an insect. Then the water was full of black smoke which came stringing out of the man's stomach. Nick pulled the blade out, and more smoke came twisting out, and the man began to sink past him, spiraling slowly as he disappeared into the murky depths, trailing blood like smoke from a downed aircraft.

Were there others? Nick glanced swiftly around, barely able to see through the sweat film that stung his eyes. Nothing moved. He stumbled upward along the coral, feeling his knees beginning to give. Yoga enabled him to hold his breath up to four minutes, but in this case the electric shock had collapsed his lungs just as he had begun the process. Now he felt a wave of blackness creeping over his vision. He sank against the coral. Water began to seep into his mouth. *No!* a voice screamed somewhere in his brain. He willed himself forward.

His shoulder hit the side of a piling as he broke the surface, but the heavy rubber took the shock of the blow. He was under a jetty. The moon and the sky and the jetty swung across his masked vision; then he pitched forward into the shallow water, swallowed the knot of saliva in his mouth and hit the release catch of the harness to free himself of the cylinder. He lay there, his mouth and nose above water, gulping down great breaths of fresh air.

It was a vulnerable moment. But no one attacked him.

After concealing his aqua-lung and flippers, Nick moved through the shadows toward the faint buzzing he knew must be the alarm. It came from a small ready-room on the jetty. The man he had just killed had been its only occupant. A half-finished cup of tea, a still smoking cigarette and Havana's Chinatown newspaper summed up his identity.

Nick studied the circuit alarm board on the wall. It

was an extremely elaborate one divided into separate ten-yard segments so that the location of the break could be pinpointed with speed and accuracy. Nick pulled the plug—and the whole circuit went dead. That would give them something to think about!

He catfooted his way up the grassy slope toward the darkened villa. It looked deserted. Had they all pulled out, leaving just one man to guard the entire island? It didn't seem likely. N3 flitted from shadow to shadow in the space of a heart beat, flattening himself first against one piece of statuary, then another. He turned and glanced up at them in the moonlight. Captain Clegg had been right! Some consisted of two figures, others of three, four, even half a dozen, but all were pornographic, their marble organs swollen out of all proportion, their satyr-like features frozen in perpetual leers. Well, everyone to his own taste, shrugged Nick. He himself preferred flesh to stone.

The ground-floor windows were locked, but one quickly gave way to Hugo's prying blade. Nick cocked his ear to one side, listening. No alarm went off. He swung himself in, landing on his bare feet like a cat. He moved across the cold tile floor, looking around, his eyes becoming accustomed to the gloom. The furniture was of bamboo, and extra large, as if built for a giant. Nick ran a finger along a huge settee. Dust an inch thick. A damp smell of plaster and decay hung in the room and in the hall beyond it. The paintings along its high walls were eighteenth-century ones, but not ancestral portraits. They, also, were pornographic—the works of such masters as Poussin, Watteau and Boucher.

All very expensive, all very luxurious—but the impression that Nick got was of an elaborate front. These rooms had never been lived in at all. They had simply been furnished, hung with pornography, then left to moulder in the damp tropical heat. Nick tried various doors that led off the long central hallway. They opened into empty, shuttered rooms.

All except one.

Nick's dark eyebrows shot up in surprise as he eased that door open.

A bank of TV monitors covered one whole wall, their

two dozen eyes staring sightlessly back at Nick. Beneath them, looking like the keyboard of a giant organ, were the switches that controlled them. Nick advanced into the room, dodging past a huge canvas chair that he saw silhouetted in the moonlight streaming in through the half-drawn blinds. His first thought was—*Judas*! He had stumbled on his headquarters!

But as he flicked on each of the monitors, Nick found himself staring at the very rooms he had just been in. Although still plunged in darkness, everything in them was quite clear. And—even more amazing—in technicolor! The second bank, numbered 11 to 23, consisted of the upstairs rooms, and these, Nick saw, were furnished and had a definitely lived-in look. In each case, the camera was pointed squarely at the bed.

Slowly it dawned on him. This was no espionage tool, but a rich man's toy. A voyeur's million-dollar electronic system employing the very latest night-shooting infrared color filters! Used, probably, to spy on guests as they enjoyed themselves with various members of A. K.'s "harem." Disgustedly, Nick started to turn away, then stopped.

The last room he had just flicked on—number 18—*was occupied*!

A giant balding tub of a man with biceps like thighs and thighs like oak logs was on the bed, leaning over a naked brunette with a delicious body meant for loving. Soft brown hair curled about her ears, and her eyes were so brown they seemed almost black. There was a dusting of pale freckles across the bridge of her nose. Her lips twisted into a wry smirk as the man's big hands cupped her magnificent breasts. He lowered himself over the girl, almost blotting her from view as he thrust her legs apart, maneuvering himself ponderously . . .

Nick was already up the stairs and counting his way along the corridor to the eighteenth room, fighting off the wave of disgust he felt. Peeping Tomism wasn't one of N3's vices—although it was often enough part of his job. He found the door and swung it open.

The girl screamed. The giant slid off her soft white body and wheeled toward Nick, unsatisfied desire still burning in him like a red-hot poker. Nick recognized him from newspaper photographs.

A. K. Atchinson was built like one of the statues in his garden. He was every Texan's idea of himself, a great beefy red bull of a man as tanned as redheads ever get. His eyes glittered at Nick with a mixture of passion and hatred, the pupils swimming strangely in their sockets as if he were drugged. N3 saw the small vial on the night table and knew with what—cantharides. Spanish fly. The giant made a lunging move toward him, and Hugo flicked into Nick's hand.

"Get dressed. Both of you," he snapped. "Unless you want to answer questions the way you are."

"Hey, are you from the mainland?" demanded the brunette eagerly. She had leaped from the bed and quickly slipped on a lacy bra and a tiny girdle that was hardly more than a garter belt with sex appeal. "My name's Kara Kane, and boy, am I glad to see you!" she bubbled enthusiastically. "There's only one thing I want—to get off this crazy, cocklemamey island!"

"You'll get off—after I get some answers," replied Nick evenly.

"Ahh, you won't get anything out of him," she said, gesturing disgustedly at A. K. as she slid a pair of sheer nylons up her legs. "He's only got one thing on his mind, and she put it there. She turned him into a human gland."

"She?"

"Ilse Smith," said Kara. "She's the one recruited me for this job. You may not believe it, but I was a pretty well-known aquatic star. I got into a narcotics jam, though, and couldn't get any more work. So when she came to me in Miami and promised me twenty Gs if I'd live out on this island with A. K. for one year—well, man, I jumped." She stood up, fastening the nylons to the girdle, and said: "Only I ain't seen a cent of it, and it's been *more* than a year and now this Ilse babe has taken a powder and I can't get my dough. *Or* get off the island!"

A.K. had subsided onto the bed. He made a soft groaning sound at the mention of Ilse's name. "She's the one he's really nuts about," laughed Kara, smoothing a dress down over her lush figure. "Says she does things for him that no one else can. I'm just a substitute until she comes back—if she comes back."

"I heard he was building Aquacity for you."

Kara gave Nick a disgusted look. "He ain't building nothing for nobody," she said. "Are you kidding? He never even leaves this room. They come here if they want him to sign a check or something."

Nick asked who *they* were.

"Ilse and a bald, creepy-looking guy. Listen, friend," she said suddenly, "I don't know what's going on here, and I don't want to know, but I'll tell you one thing. I've watched that dame turn this poor bastard into a vegetable over the last fourteen months. Okay, maybe he was a lecherous old goat to begin with. But he was also a damn shrewd operator who was running the whole show for himself. Now look at him! It's pitiful!"

"This Ilse," demanded Nick suddenly. "What's she look like?"

"I'll do better than tell you," said Kara Kane, leaning across the bed and pushing a button. A movie projector slid out of the night table, its lens pointed at the ceiling. She pressed another button and it began to project an image. Nick had to crane his neck to make it out. It was in technicolor—technique number one-oh-five, sometimes called the Thirsty Mare, a bedroom trick which sometimes called for a third party. There were only two in this case, though. A. K. and—

Ingra Brand!

"She's actually a blonde," Kara Kane was saying, "but A. K. likes brunettes, so she wears a wig when she's with him."

"How long has she been away from here?"

"About three weeks now."

It was all falling into place. Now Nick knew which of the twins was really Ingra, which Ilse. The one on the beach off No Name Causeway that night—*that* had been Ilse. Years before, Nick had masqueraded as a sailor visiting a Chinese port and had allowed himself to be lured into a place called The Heaven of a Thousand and One Delights. Its inhabitants were ladies of the night, specially trained to use their wiles on visiting seamen and foreign officials to compromise them into working for the Red Chinese cause. China's spy trainees went there, too, to learn the seductive arts and how best to use them on their chosen targets.

That night on the beach! What a blind fool he'd been not to recognize those techniques that "Ingra Brand" —actually Ilse Lautenbach—had used on him!

Nick glanced down at A. K. Atchinson. He was writhing on the bed as he watched the film unfold on the ceiling, his lips forming and reforming the name "Ilse." Nick had to turn away. It was more than he could take. How many men had this modern Circe turned into swine? She had certainly enslaved this one. Perhaps she had enslaved Ochoa, too—before killing him. Then he thought of the real Ingra. Could she possibly be on Peligro, brought here as a prisoner? He said to Kara Kane: "Look, I'll see that you get off this island—if you cooperate with me."

"Sure. What can I do?"

"Where are the women's quarters?"

She laughed. "There's no harem here, believe me. I wish there was. There's just little old me, sore as all get out."

"O.K. No women," he chuckled. "But earlier today I saw men—lots of them. Where are they now?"

"Come on," she said, "I'll show you where the action is." Nick glanced back at Atchinson. "Don't worry," she said, "he'll be okay as long as the movie's on."

And so they left A. K. to his solitary pleasures.

Kara led Nick downstairs and out across a moonlit garden aflame with hibiscus, bougainvillaea and roses. She stopped at a white latticework gazebo which stood on the lawn, commanding a view of distant palms, a crescent of white sand and the ocean beyond. She pulled a couple of garden chairs aside and pressed something with her foot. The stone foundation swung silently aside, revealing a circular, polished metal shaft as large as the gazebo itself. Nick leaned forward, peering down it. A blast of hot, metallic air came wafting up, and he saw an elevator rising toward them.

"Whatever they're up to," said Kara, "it's going on down there. I've never gone down myself," she added. "It's off-limits to me, but still—I see them come and go." The elevator rose into the gazebo and stopped with a soft swoosh. Nick was about to step into it, but she grabbed his arm. "You go down this way," she said, "and you'll be right in their laps. I know another way—unguarded. Come on."

She led him back into the villa and downstairs to the cellar. "This is the way they come when they want to visit A. K.," she said, and pulled back a wine shelf. Nick tugged the trap door open. An iron-rung ladder led down into a brilliantly lit passageway. "You're a sweetheart," murmured Nick, kissing her on her cute, freckled nose.

She moved up against him, running her hands over his muscles. "You feel pretty strong under your rubber," she laughed. "I wish we had time."

"So do I," chuckled Nick. "Maybe when I come back up. Meanwhile, wait here in the house with A. K. I shouldn't be gone long. If I am, try to make it to the mainland on your own."

"You make it sound dangerous," she said. "And all along I thought they were running a Chinese laundry down there."

Nick grinned and descended into CLAW's subterranean nerve center, closing the trap door after him.

He had taken only about 12 paces down the passageway when a voice behind him suddenly shouted, "Halt!"

N3 whirled around, Hugo flicking out, ready.

When he saw what faced him, though, he dropped the stiletto and slowly raised both hands over his head.

Chapter 15

If there had been two men, three or four, even half a dozen, N3 would have taken them on. But 24 masked figures faced him, standing in a double column. Twenty-five, actually, counting the one in the lead who held the submachine gun on him.

They hadn't been there a second ago—but Nick saw the half-open ventilation tunnel out of which they had just stepped, its cover the same polished zinc sheeting as the walls of the passageway itself.

"Keep your hands up. Walk slowly toward me," ordered the figure with the machine gun. As he spoke, the twanging echo of what sounded like a throat amplifier moaned and screeched along the passageway.

Nick advanced toward the group. As he did, he immediately noticed some interesting differences between the leader and the column behind him. For one thing, he was the only one armed. For another, their hands were behind their backs. For a third, their wet suits were orange, while his was black and had extra equipment slung from it—keys, underwater torch, what looked like a steel billy club.

With each step he took, Nick became increasingly certain that he wasn't facing 25 enemies, but only *one* enemy guarding 24 possible allies! The men's features were all concealed by bulky oxygen rebreathers, but N3 was willing to bet that only one would prove to be Chinese.

He was only a couple of paces from the leader now, and with the advantage of already having his hands over his head. He pretended to trip, then caught himself. At least his bottom half. His raised hands had actually gathered

125

speed, and they came down now in a rigid, lethal blur, slamming into the man's shoulders like the cutting edges of twin axes. The submachine gun dropped, unfired, from his grasp. The rattling choke of pain was amplified horribly by his throat mike. Even as he fell, Killmaster followed up with another ax-blade blow to the side of his neck that snapped it with a whiplash crack. The man crumpled to the floor, dead.

N3 crouched, ready to take on any of the other 24 who moved toward him. None of them did. The first figure to the right turned slightly so that Nick saw the handcuffs and the chain that was passed through them, linking him to the others. Nick ripped the key from the guard's body and quickly unlocked the cuffs. The man pulled his hands free, rubbed his wrists, and then unclipped the oxygen rebreather from his face. As Nick had guessed, he was American—lantern-jawed, with a stubble of blond beard and piercing blue eyes.

Nick started to speak, but the man quickly put his fingers to his lips and motioned him toward the ventilating shaft. "My name's Baker," he whispered hoarsely over the steady roar of machinery in the shaft. "No time to lose. TV monitors everywhere. If we don't check past the one down the tunnel in another minute, they'll send a search party up after us." He glanced around, as if on the lookout for a hidden mike, then said: "Put on the guard's wet suit! He was a big Korean—about your size. Then you lead us. I'll tell you where to go, what to do. Each work party is connected to the leader by Bendix marine radio system. Runs on batteries, uses throat mikes. Come on."

They pulled the guard's body into the ventilating shaft, and Nick stripped off his own wet suit and put on the guard's. "We can talk on this system without being overheard," said Baker, "as long as you don't press either of these two buttons." And he pointed to a couple on Nick's belt. "This one amplifies your voice through the rebreather and this red one hooks you into the main communication circuit. Above all, don't press that one—unless they buzz you. And let's hope to God they don't."

Nick transferred Pierre to his new wet suit and retrieved Hugo, after which the two men concealed the guard's body and the other wet suit in an air funnel.

Then they set out in their double column down the passageway with Nick, submachine gun in hand, leading the way.

"Here's the monitor," crackled Baker's voice in his ear. "You won't see it. It's hidden. Raise your right hand, thumb and forefinger touching, forming a circle. That's the okay sign." Nick did. "Okay, now a right turn into this shaft."

It was of circular, polished metal and dropped away slightly, stretching ahead, featureless except for the ridges where the sections of pipe joined. As they moved along it, Baker's voice continued to crackle information into Nick's ear. They were a work party, he said, just going on shift, but they had stopped to do a brief repair job on the ventilating system. They had temporarily cut the air supply off while working, hence the rebreathers, and as they were now heading into what he called the "Vacuum tube" there was no point in taking them off.

"Question," said Nick. "Are you men the original divers who contracted out to build Aquacity?"

"You bet your sweet life we are," replied Baker, "but whatever the hell we're building, it ain't no Aquacity. I hope you're from the government," he added. Nick said that in a way he was. "It's about time you people tumbled to what's going on down here," said Baker bitterly. "We've been locked up in this trap for over a year. Nearly a hundred of us! Okay, here comes another monitor now. Do what you did before, then make a left into the next cross tunnel."

Air from the ventilating system blew past them. Canned stuff, from the air-conditioning plant, Baker explained as they moved along the cross tunnel. "What gets me," his voice crackled, "is that the whole thing was built by Americans, *us,* with American equipment that was supposed to go into Aquacity! There's only about sixty of them to a hundred of us, but the whole setup is so automated and interconnected with closed-circuit TV that we can't even blow our noses that they don't know about it. Until you killed that guard, we didn't have a Chinaman's chance. Ha! That's good!"

The air was getting warmer in the shaft. There was a smell of heat in the air, metallic heat. Nick began to sweat under the rubber. "We'll be coming out in the main control room in a minute," Baker's voice said. "Just do what I tell you and we'll be okay. There's only one place I've found where they can't see or hear us," he added, "but we won't hit it until we come back from the work shift."

As they continued down the sloping shaft, Baker told Nick that the divers' first mistake had been signing a contract that compelled them to remain on Peligro a year. "Because of that, nobody came looking for us," he said disgustedly. "The Chinks let us write letters but they read them all and they made us rewrite them if it looked like we were giving anything away. So most of us just gave up writing." At first, Baker added, the setup had looked normal enough. "It took us about six weeks to figure out we weren't building Aquacity, and by then it was too late. They had us boxed in, but good. Okay, watch it!" his voice suddenly crackled urgently. "Here we are!"

The vaulted subterranean chamber into which they emerged was divided down the middle by a thick pane of glass. Behind it were banks of monitors, dials, flashing controls and triple rows of pushbutton switches, a huge computer unit, and five figures in white, sitting in a row like the control team in a missile tracking station.

"That's the big cheese," Baker's metallic voice rasped in Nick's earphones. "All the way over on the left." But N3 didn't need to be told. The patchwork face, the weird smile, the flesh-colored gloves, the high-pitched voice—all were as familiar to him as the back of his own hands.

Judas!

He was issuing instructions over the P.A. system to a cluster of white-gowned technicians on the other side of the glass who were working on various sections of a submarine. The sub—a bulbous, blunt-nosed, football-like object—was cradled in a complicated superstructure of steel piping inside what looked like a huge, waterless bathtub. Baker's voice said: "They brought in Chink technicians to work on this baby. I understand they got them as far as Cuba disguised as oil refinery experts—but it beats me how they got them into the U.S."

"Looks atomic powered," said Nick.

"It is. Don't stop to look at it, though. Keep going toward that third elevator shaft on the left. We go down in that to the next level." He paused. "See the old geezer in the wheelchair next to the top banana?" he asked. Nick had seen him, all right—Professor Brand. "This is his brainchild," said Baker. "I've heard the Chinks boast that it can travel indefinitely at depths of up to six thousand feet because of some atomic rheostat the old bird invented. I'll tell you something else they *didn't* tell us, but I saw it for myself. This baby has a vertical launching tube for a missile. A couple of us watched them test the mechanism the other day. The sub stops—say, six thousand feet down—and holds dead steady. They've got the target pinned down by radio fixes and a star-tracker periscope. They feed it all into the missile's brain, then press a button and the missile shoots up through the water by compressed air. The solid-fuel rockets ignite as it breaks the surface and its track is corrected. Then, whamo!"

They were in the elevator now. The doors slid shut and Baker said, "Press the bottom button." Nick had sighted Dr. Orff sitting beside Brand in the glassed-in control booth, together with two other men, both of whom had occidental features but wore the visored caps and denim uniforms of guards. Nick asked about them. "Maybe they're Americans, maybe they're not," said Baker. "All I know is they speak Chinese. I think they're his guards. They showed up with him yesterday. You know, I can't figure this Brand guy out. The Chinks have had a lot of trouble with him, I hear. Until yesterday they wouldn't even bring him out here. They kept him on Big Pine. He designed this whole setup on paper—and I mean everything. The sub, the control station, the vacuum tube. The guy's some kind of genius. But I hear he's been balking every step of the way. That's why this whole thing has taken so long. They've tried everything on him—brainwashing, threatening his daughter, but he's still dragging his feet. You know," he added, "we're only hours away from the big moment." Nick swung toward him, about to ask exactly how many hours away and of what it would consist, but the elevator doors slid silently open. "Break radio contact now," said Baker. "We're going into the tube."

Two guards wearing rebreathers signaled Nick to un-hook his men from the chain that linked them. When he had done so, the entire group was herded into a long circular decompression chamber. A tube-shaped train about the size of an average city sewer pipe sat waiting for them in a smooth aluminum depression. The men were strapped into it, lying out flat, one behind the other, in separate plastic compartments that resembled a string of hot dogs. Nick was the last one in.

After the guards had strapped him in, one of them flicked a switch at the control board. The train suddenly began to move, accelerating to fantastic speed within seconds. Nick fought to tear open his eyes against the tremendous pressure forcing them shut. They were trav-eling through the aluminum tubing with the speed and smoothness of a bullet fired along a rifle's bore. No more than 60 seconds could have elapsed when he suddenly felt the "train" slowing—plunging, as it were, into a soft pillow of air.

The process was then repeated. Guards unstrapped them and herded them through the decompression cham-ber—only this time they were not rechained. "Radio contact okay again," crackled Baker's voice. "You lead us straight ahead through the tunnel. But watch yourself. They have monitors here, too."

The tunnel climbed steeply through what appeared to be solid coral. Inspection lights in the stone ceiling glowed dimly through the heavy haze of coral dust. An overhead conveyor belt was hurrying a river of pulverized coral past them, but although the clanking of its rollers should have been deafening, Nick heard no noise at all.

"Where are we?" he asked.

"Twenty-six miles northeast of Peligro," Baker's voice replied. "What did you think of the vacuum tube?" he asked, a touch of pride in his voice. "Brand may have developed the original idea, but we built it. The idea is simplicity itself—air let in one end of a vacuum tube will project whatever is inside it at the speed of a bullet. A little air meeting it will slow down the object. It took us six months to lay the piping for that thing. . . ."

"Under the ocean's surface, of course," said Nick, remembering Brand's English Channel invasion plan.

"That's right," replied Baker. "Through sand for about twenty miles, solid rock for the last six. It's a real engineering feat. I figure there must be some kind of base they're trying to reach above us."

Nick said nothing, but his features were grim beneath his mask. They were under a base, all right. The Cape Sable missile base! And they had gotten there simply by burrowing *beneath* all the elaborate underwater warning devices that NASA Security had so proudly demonstrated for him!

Up ahead, Nick saw a 24-man team working with high-speed compression drills, boring their way through the solid rock. Again, where there should have been unbelievable noise there was only an eerie silence. He asked Baker about it as they approached the checkpoint.

"You notice the air kind of vibrating against you?" Baker's voice crackled in his ear. Nick said he did. "Well, that's what does it. Electric current is carried through wires to a device called an audifier, where it's converted to radio frequency power at 20,000 cycles a second, and this is transformed into mechanical energy, or vibrations, which swallow up the original sound. The vibrations themselves get bounced and rebounced off these walls until I guess they don't show up on any of the instruments that they may have above. Okay, watch yourself here," he continued, his voice suddenly urgent. "Just say *dungshi* to the guard. It's our shift now. We'll be working the drills for the next three hours—and don't hesitate to smack us with your billy from time to time for realism's sake."

They were about an hour into the shift when the buzzer on Nick's belt suddenly went off. He swung around. The chief technician was waving him over to the small canvas leanto from which he'd been directing the drilling operations. Nick approached, pressing the red button which linked him into the main communication circuit. While operating in Peking some years earlier, N3 had picked up enough Mandarin to be able to carry on a fairly extensive conversation. He just hoped the chief technician wasn't a North Korean.

He wasn't. Mandarin trickled into Nick's earphones. "The Big One wishes to speak with you," the man said, gesturing toward the monitor. Nick turned. *Judas was staring at him from the screen!* Was it a two-way view? he wondered with alarm. The weirdly twisted mouth on the screen began to move, and the familiar voice keened like an excited mosquito in his earphones.

"You will bring your group back immediately," Judas said in rapid, colloquial Mandarin. "The chief engineer has announced that we are now less than ten inches from breakthrough into the missile silo. After you have escorted your work party to the cell blocks you will report back to the compression chamber and join the special assault party setting out. Things will have been made ready, meanwhile, in the silo itself." A mechanical-looking hand dismissed Nick.

On the way back to Peligro in the vacuum tube, Nick's mind was racing wildly. To judge from the size of the tunnel through which they were once again hurtling it seemed obvious that CLAW didn't plan to steal the entire PHO missile, just its specialized computer brain—a complex electronic mass no larger than an ordinary automobile engine. This they would probably connect to their own warhead in Brand's super-submarine. To cover up the theft of the missile brain and to give them time to reach the unassailable depths of the Atlantic they probably planned to blow up the Cape Sable silo. Radiation would then make it impossible for anyone to enter it for 48 hours.

By the time the theft of the missile brain was discovered, *Red China would be dictating terms to the rest of the World!*

As Nick led his 24-man group from the compression chamber on Peligro, a plan was growing in his mind. He could handle things at this end; he just hoped Julie would be able to deal with Ilse Lautenbach at her's. To Baker he said, "Let me know when we reach that blind spot in the monitor system."

But it was not Baker's voice that trickled a reply into Nick's earphones. "Agent N3 of AXE," the thin, high-pitched voice of Judas lashed out. "The body of the guard has just been discovered in Ventilating Tunnel Seven. Look around you, then carefully place your submachine gun at your feet. Resistance is useless."

Nick spun around. A steel door slid smoothly across the tunnel entrance behind him, while from the other direction a column of guards advanced with drawn submachine guns.

Chapter 16

The countdown had begun at Cape Sable.

The radar scanners faced southeastward, toward Ascension Island, 5,000 miles away. The lights were blinking on the big board in Central Control as a medley of voices in charge of telemetering, guidance and destruction merged and separated on the P.A. system.

Julie Baron stood flattened against the wall of the main blockhouse, watching Ilse Lautenbach march briskly across the concrete apron toward the guard gate. The huge gantry and saucer-shaped reflectors beyond were clearly outlined in the moonlight, and a thin, ghostly wisp of steam rose from the silo, now connected by a thick cable with the launching site.

The iron voice of the P.A. boomed out the countdown from atop every building: "Twenty-seven hours, sixteen minutes, thirty seconds . . . telemeter contact . . . tank pressure okay . . . gyros okay . . . rocket-tank pressure correct . . ."

Julie saw the two uniformed guards barring Ilse's way. They kept pointing to the red warning light flashing on the gantry, and the sign which hung from the fence. It said: NO PERSONNEL BEYOND THIS POINT AFTER COUNTDOWN HAS BEGUN.

Ilse reached into the bulky handbag she carried, as if searching for identification. Suddenly both guards crumpled. Ilse glanced quickly about, then hurried on toward the silo.

Julie moved out of the shadows in pursuit.

The frozen expressions on the guards' faces suggested nerve gas—probably carried in an ordinary plastic nasal

134

spray bottle. Julie hurried on, darting from shadow to shadow. She saw Ilse disappear down the iron-runged ladder that curved around the silo's walls. Julie moved forward to the edge and peered down. From the floor, 50 feet below, the circular wall of polished metal rose like a gigantic gun barrel. She watched Ilse moving down the steps, slowly circling the great glistening chromium projectile which rested on a blunt cone of latticed steel. Near its base, Ilse stepped over the rail, walked gingerly along the gantry's narrow bridge, opened a small access door and disappeared inside the projectile itself.

Julie slipped off her shoes and hurried down the curving iron ladder. There was no time to get help. She was sure Ilse had tools in that bulky handbag, and from the quick, sure way she moved it was obvious she knew exactly what she was doing. A few turns of a screwdriver here, a few there—and God alone knew what she could to the PHO's control system.

It took Julie about five minutes to get the access door open. For a terrible moment she was afraid Ilse had locked it from inside; but it was only jammed. The first thing Julie saw as she swung it open was the handbag. It lay half open on the smooth chromium flooring, precision tools scattered about carelessly. Ilse herself stood balanced at the top of an iron ladder, some five feet above her, disconnecting a complicated series of wires. Probably the warning system. The tight black dress she wore had no pockets, so Julie didn't have to worry about the nerve gas. It would still be in the handbag.

Ilse almost toppled from her perch as the access door clanged shut behind Julie. "Who are you?" she cried. "What are you doing here? This area is closed to unauthorized personnel."

"Better come down, dear," said Julie sweetly as she kicked the handbag out of reach. "The game's up, as they say."

Ilse came down—but not as expected. Her skirt billowed around her thighs as she plummeted the distance, landing on her bare feet like a cat, her cunning sharp eyes sliding sideways, measuring the inches toward the handbag, her hands curling into claws. She looked as if she was about to spring. Instead, her foot snaked out, catching Julie square in the stomach. As she staggered backward, Ilse followed up with a swinging fist to the side of Julie's head that sent her sprawling across the smooth chrome.

Julie shook her head, momentarily stunned. She saw Ilse's foot come flashing at her face, grabbed the ankle and sank her teeth into the instep. Ilse screamed, trying to wrench free. Too late. Julie jackknifed to one knee, the foot still in her hands. She heaved upward and Ilse's other foot left the floor and she crashed full length.

Her hands scrabbled toward the handbag. Julie dived on top of her, clawing and tearing. Ilse's hand snaked up, caught the neck of Julie's dress and split it down to the hem. Her fingers hooked around the bra, pulled, and Julie's abundant breasts spilled free. Ilse's head jerked forward, her lips bared from her teeth. Julie screamed as the other girl's teeth sank into her breast. She fell backward, trying to protect herself, and Ilse staggered to her feet, her own breasts bursting free from the torn bodice of her dress.

They were both on their feet now, circling each other warily. The heat inside the projectile was intense, and Ilse tore away the remnants of her dress, letting it fall about her feet and stepping out of it. Julie did the same, for her dress was hampering her movements. They continued to circle, Ilse trying to maneuver her way toward the handbag. Both girls were panting, their breasts heaving, and a thin sheen of sweat covered their naked, exquisite bodies.

Suddenly Ilse lunged forward, hands coming together like a vise. Julie's left foot lashed out in a savage karate kick that echoed through the projectile like a pistol shot. Ilse screamed, clutched at herself and fell to her knees. Her hands went up to protect her face—but too late. Julie was already astride her, forcing her onto her back, her long, elegant fingers raking Ilse's face and breasts.

WHAM! The access door suddenly burst open behind her. Julie swung around, started to say, "Well, it's about time somebody gave me a hand," but the words froze in her throat.

There was no mistaking the yellowish, Oriental fold of the eyes above the oxygen rebreather, no doubt about the language that squawked out of the chest speaker. *"Loy gee, ar koo lar!* Hurry up, grab them!"

Two masked figures in black wet suits leaped through the access door, pulling Julie off Ilse's bloody, naked body. More figures in black rubber suits came hurrying through the door behind them, carrying tools. They clambered up the ladder, and an acetylene torch blazed into life. There were terse commands, the sound of wrenches and screwdrivers turning. Sparks showered down.

Ilse was on her feet now, her eyes blazing hatred at Julie. "Leave her here!" she spat out in Mandarin. "Let her blow up with it!"

"I recognize this one!" rasped the voice box. "I saw her in Peking not three weeks ago."

Julie twisted in his grasp, studying the slanted eyes above the rebreather. No doubt about it—it was Lo Jui-ching of the MPS Fifth Bureau, Armed Counterespionage. *"Tew nar ma!"* she spat out. It was the venomous epithet of hatred and scorn that no Chinese can ever forgive.

The eyes above the rebreather hardened. "No, she comes with us," the voice box rasped. "There are more interesting ways of dying than in explosions."

"But that will mean leaving someone else behind," protested Ilse.

A blade suddenly flicked through the air, plunging into a black rubber suit. The technician fell to his knees in agony, feeling in back for the thing that hurt him. "His part was finished," said the voice box. The man couldn't quite reach the blade, and he sighed and fell forward onto his face. "Take his rebreather. Give it to the girl."

The four men carrying the missile's electronic brain carefully stepped over the body and backed out the access door, grunting instructions at each other.

As Julie was led across the gantry and down the remaining steps of the ladder, she saw a demolition team hurriedly stringing wires between charges that had been placed at strategic locations around the silo. She also saw the discolored, oyster-hued zinc at the silo's base, and the great gaping hole that had been burned through it by the powerful acetylene torches. The metal was still hot and scorched her bare feet as she was forced to walk across it. Then the masked figures were pulling her down into the hot, stinking bowels of the earth itself. . . .

Nick glanced around and saw the steel door slide across the tunnel entrance, sealing him and his 24-man work party inside the cell blocks. From the other direction, meanwhile, a column of guards approached, their submachine guns drawn. Nick didn't put down his own gun as Judas had ordered, however. In the narrow tunnel the advantage was with him. The enemy column advanced two abreast—which meant that only the first two could fire without hitting those in front.

N3's response was too quick for them. Judas' voice was still keening in his earphones as he pressed the trigger. The submachine gun bucked and jumped in his arms like a living thing. The first two guards were hurled backward as if they had been kicked. They slammed into those behind, throwing off their aim. Nick swerved the m.g. up at the overhead bulbs. They dissolved into darkness, leaving the guards silhouetted against the light from the cell blocks behind them.

"The keys!" barked Baker's voice in his earphones. N3 tore them from his belt and handed them to him. Judas' voice broke in now, saying, "You will gain nothing by this, N3. Put down your arms." Baker's voice came in over his, drowning him out. "Get the monitor!" it yelled. "In the far corner, overhead!" Nick aimed at that spot and pulled the trigger. Judas' voice broke up into a distorted squawk of noise that was abruptly sliced off by a second burst.

A couple of the guards came leaping over their slain companions, flame stabbing from their guns. Nick hit the floor, firing, as bullets whistled past him. The first guard clutched at his neck and spun slowly around. The second doubled over, shot in the stomach. Echoes of gunfire thundered slowly up and down the tunnel. Nick saw men rushing past him now, charging toward the guards. He glanced over his shoulder. Baker was hurrying along the column, unlocking handcuffs, pulling the chain free. "There's only one other monitor!" his voice crackled in Nick's earphones. "In the cell block itself. But the boys there will know how to take care of that!"

The first of the charging divers was cut down by gunfire. The one right behind him managed to reach the first of the dead guards, however, grabbed his submachine gun and returned the fire. Those behind him each seized guns. Within seconds, the entire column of guards had been wiped out—at a cost of only two divers. They now charged into the cell blocks, and Nick set about unlocking the other prisoners. All the work shifts were in. That meant that, all told, they were now close to a hundred strong. But what good would it do? They were still sealed inside the cell blocks.

"But not for long," snapped N3. "I've got an idea."

The heavy, not quite human hand reached out across the bank of multicolored dials and switches. A mechanical-looking finger slowly unfolded, then suddenly stabbed down, pressing the small red button all the way into the panel. There was no noise in the central control booth—but the two men sitting inside it smiled in vicarious enjoyment at the explosion that they knew was tearing the Cape Sable silo apart.

"And that," said Judas with satisfaction, "is that."

He was staring through the glass at the PHO missile's electronic brain which, at that moment, was being gingerly carried from the subterranean elevator by four guards.

Dr. Karl Orff turned toward Judas and said in German: "What is happening now in the cell blocks?"

The weird, stitched-on smile twisted into a grimace of disgust. "Bah! Who knows?" the thin voice lashed out. "They have cut off the monitors. But there is no time to worry about them now. They are sealed in, and we have much to do. Call Brand and see if he has completed the adjustments inside the submarine. There is not a moment to lose."

"And the two women?" asked Orff, gesturing toward Ilse and Julie, who stood beneath the control booth among the black-suited guards.

"Get them both out of here!" snapped Judas. "Ilse should return to her post upstairs. We don't want that fool Atchinson in our hair at the last moment. As for the other one, do with her as you wish."

Orff picked up a mike and issued instructions. Ilse Lautenbach nodded and headed toward the bank of elevators. Two guards, holding Julie between them, followed her into one of them and the doors slid shut.

Professor Brand reported everything in readiness and, moments later, he emerged from the submarine's hatch and was helped down the swinging steel gangway by two guards. He looked pale and drawn, and moved with great difficulty despite their aid and the malacca cane on which he leaned. "Carry him!" ordered Judas. "Precious time is slipping through our fingers."

When Brand was back inside the control booth, Judas pulled a switch and seawater came pouring into the berth in which the submarine rested. It crashed against the glass partition in heavy green waves. When it had completely covered the submarine, Judas pressed a button and the steel superstructure fell away from beneath it. "Is the wet team ready?" he barked.

"Wet team ready, sir," came the answer in Mandarin from the group of 40 men in masks, flippers and oxygen rebreathers who stood before the control booth.

"Is the missile component ready?"

"Waterproofed and ready, sir," crackled the answer over the P.A.

"Very well, load the component aboard the sled," snapped Judas. He turned to Brand. "What's the pressure now?"

"Thirty-seven pounds per square inch," replied Brand in a weak, quavering voice. "Equal to the sea pressure outside."

"Good. We'll open the hatch," replied Judas. His claw-like fingers closed stiffly around a switch and drew it back. A great steel partition at the far end of the berth slid slowly open and schools of darting fish paused to peer out of the dark ocean depths at the curious steel fish which now came nosing out of its berth to join them.

Judas leaned toward his mike and threw a switch. "Do you receive me, Captain Li Tsu?" he barked, glancing up toward one of the monitor screens. It flickered to life, and a Chinese face in a visored cap and turtle-neck sweater appeared on it. "Awaiting your orders, sir," came the reply in Mandarin.

"Take her down to the ocean floor," ordered Judas. "Open your forward hatch and flood the missile tube." He glanced at the wet team waiting in the glassed-in compression chamber as the water rose slowly over them. "The sled with the component is on its way."

Nick Carter cursed savagely. "They've got the PHO's electronic brain!" he growled, watching CLAW's wet team fan out around the battery-powered underwater sled, face masks gleaming, fluttering fins kicking out behind as they swam out of the compression chamber and into the dark ocean depths in perfect formation.

He switched off the monitor with a heavy heart, knowing that CLAW's possession of the component meant two things—that Julie must have been killed and the Cape Sable installation blown sky high. He turned to Jim Baker and the 22 other divers who stood with him in their wet suits and rebreathers in the vacuum tube's compression chamber. "Is there a direct exit into the ocean from here?" he asked tensely. "One that you might have used when you were constructing the tube from Peligro to Sable?"

Baker was silent a moment. "The pressure would be terrific," he mused, "but we could blast our way out. We've got the charges," he said, gesturing toward the guards' ready room, "and I know the weakest point in the compression chamber. It's where we soldered up the old access door we used to use."

"Well, we've come this far," said Nick. "Let's go for broke."

Getting out of the cell block had been comparatively easy. Nick himself was already in a guard's uniform; so it had simply been a matter of having Baker and the others don the uniforms, rebreathers and face masks of the guards they had killed, and then of approaching the steel door that sealed them off. Nick had banged on it with the muzzle of his submachine gun and shouted in perfect Mandarin: "Open up, comrades. We've dealt with the imperialist swine in here. Give us a hand with their bodies." The guards in the vacuum tube's compression chamber had immediately slid the door open —and died in a hail of bullets.

The next problem they'd had to overcome was that there were not enough wet suits and rebreathers to go around. Baker had come up with the solution to that. Send the 70-odd prisoners they'd released straight to Peligro's surface through the ventilating tubes and the trapdoor that opened into A. K. Atchinson's villa. There were few guards topside, and the men could ready the hydrofoils and anything else that floated, and have them waiting for them.

Now, as Baker set up the explosive charges, Nick distributed knives, flippers and spear guns to everyone from the guards' ready room, saying: "Remember, men, when it blows we're going to come out fast and, let's hope, in one piece. It will take a moment or so to get our bearings. Look for the sub first. The sled will be on its way toward it. The idea is to get the sled away from them and up to the surface, then load it aboard one of the hydrofoils and hightail it out of here. Don't stop for anything else—such as personal revenge on guards," he added meaningfully. "There won't be time."

It was like being hurled through space inside a rubber ball.

The thick pillow of air in which they were embedded protected them somewhat from the blast, and the tons of seawater which came bursting through the gaping hole where the access door had been scooped them up and out into the ocean, carrying them toward the surface at terrific speed. As it started to break up, the balloon of air rushed past them and hit the bubbling and swirling surface with the impact of a bomb.

Nick felt himself being tumbled through the water like a spinning top. There was a sharp pain in his ears. He fought with his fins to slow down, to get decompression. Behind him, 20-odd projectiles came shooting up through the burst of silver air bubbles. There were also a couple that were already floating back toward the ocean floor in the unmistakable postures of death.

Nick felt a tap on his shoulder. It was Jim Baker, motioning toward his ears. The communication system had gone dead, knocked out by the blast. Baker pointed down into the gloom. Nick saw the silvery bulge of the sub on the ocean floor, and the wedge of black-suited divers swimming down toward it with the sled. They wore bulky cylinders between their aqua-lungs, he saw—compressed-air packs that gave them twice the speed of his own group. This was offset, however, by the weight of the missile component, which caused their battery-operated sled to move sluggishly. N3 grinned. Those air packs would actually do nothing but help his own men distinguish friend from foe!

Nick's arm swept forward, signaling attack. As they closed in on the CLAW wet team, he saw the CO_2 guns slung from their waists and extra spears strapped to their legs. The leader's mask swung up, sighting them. Immediately the others glanced around. They had the advantage of being in radio contact with one another. But Nick's group had the greater advantage of being above and behind them, with the early morning glare of the surface in the enemy's eyes.

Nick flung himself forward, his blue shark knife streaming out ahead of him like a lance. It caught the nearest CLAWman in the hip, hurling him against the one next to him. Nick drove in the knife, wrenching it from side to side. The man dropped his CO_2 gun as blood threaded blackly from the wound. He doubled up, water pouring into his mouth around the edges of the rebreather.

Nick had the knife out and was churning forward again into the midst of the wildly scattering figures. To his right he saw Baker wrestling with a black-suited figure, and tearing off his face mask. Above and to his left, more of his divers were locked in mortal combat with CLAWmen. A figure in a jet pack went down in front of Nick, clawing at his face, the glass of his mask smashed, his face hideously contorted.

N3 glanced around and spotted the sled with its precious rubber-packed cargo. It was guarded by two CLAWmen, their CO_2 guns ready. Nick dug his foot against a lump of coral and, with this to give him leverage, lunged forward. A stream of bubbles exploded from one of the guns and a spear ripped into the rubber protecting his shoulder. He felt pain and wetness that could either be blood or water. He dodged another flash of metal, and pulled the trigger of his own gun. The spear caught the nearest guard in the neck and he somersaulted backward in slow motion, turning over and sinking toward the ocean floor, kicking feebly, black smoke bubbling from his throat.

The other guard was on him now. The butt of a CO_2 gum slammed into Nick's head, momentarily stunning him. The man was pulling at his rebreather now, his elbow crashing again and again into Nick's mask, trying to break it. Hugo flicked into N3's free hand, and he drove it home into the yellowish square of flesh above the rubber suit. The man's face contorted hideously inside his mask, and he thrashed away from Nick, kicking his way through insane loops like a plane gone out of control, black smoke threading from an ugly wound beneath his ear.

Nick swung back toward the sled. Baker and six other divers now had it in their possession, he saw, and were steering it toward the surface. Baker turned, giving him the finger-circle okay sign. N3 glanced around. Here and there, black-suited figures were sinking slowly toward the ocean floor amid a tangle of spears, strips of black rubber, aqua-lungs and CO_2 guns. He saw the great gray flanks of carnivores already beginning to move among them, fins twitching at the sight of so much blood.

It was time to clear out! He kicked his way upward, following the other dim shapes through the milky turbulence left by the battle. Nick took a last look below as he hung 20 feet beneath the surface, treading water, waiting for the decompression pain in his ears to end. The submarine still rested among coral clumps on the sandy bottom, seemingly an inanimate object. N3 smiled grimly. He'd give more than a pretty penny to hear the messages flashing back and forth between its captain and Judas now!

Then Nick turned and jackknifed his way up the remaining 20 feet. As his head broke the surface, he pulled off the rebreather and face mask and took deep, lung-filling breaths of the blessed, sweet-smelling air. . . .

There wasn't long to enjoy it. Bullets were already lacing into the water, raising tiny geysers on all sides. "They grabbed one of the hydrofoils!" yelled Baker. He and his men were manhandling the missile brain, sled and all, into a waiting hydrofoil. Nick swam toward them in long, slicing strokes. He glanced over his shoulder and saw the big silver grasshopper bearing down on the jetty, flame stabbing from its forward guns.

"Quick!" he yelled. "Man that recoilless rifle aft!"

As he swung aboard he saw A. K. Atchinson and Kara Kane being helped aboard the next hydrofoil over. "Listen," he shouted to Baker over the roaring cough of the 57mm gun, "you better get those two out of here. Take that other hydrofoil out. I'll cover you from here."

Baker yelled, "When those other guys hit daylight they went nuts. The bastards didn't even wait for us. They just took off in anything that would float—two-man subs, underwater chariots. They couldn't figure out the controls on these hydrofoils or they would have taken them, too. The bastards!"

"You can't blame them!" yelled Nick. "Hey, watch out for the back blast on that baby!" he added, for Baker had hoisted the recoilless rifle onto his shoulder and the propellant gases were escaping from a breech only inches from his face.

"Don't worry," grinned Baker, "I handled one of these at Chongchon, in Korea."

A direct hit on the forward deck of the enemy's hydrofoil sent flame and debris mushrooming skyward. The craft careened away, motors screaming full out. "Nice shooting, buddy," said Nick. "They'll be back, though, and with reinforcements. When I reconnoitered this island I saw a whole base of these things over on the other side. Listen!" He held up his finger. The distant roar of motors could be heard approaching from around the promontory. "Better get going!" Nick yelled. "I'm going to take the missile component in alone. I don't want anyone with me. Too dangerous."

"Okay, friend," said Baker, shaking Nick's hand. He vaulted onto the deck of the other hydrofoil. "Good luck. Maybe I can create a bit of diversion for you."

"If you can, fine," said Nick. "Give Kara Kane my thanks," he yelled as the other hydrofoil pulled away, "and tell her maybe next time." Baker grinned and waved, and then he was gone, the craft rising out of the storm of its own vapor like a great bird.

Nick climbed into the control cockpit of his own hydrofoil and set about familiarizing himself with the vast bank of buttons and switches. The thing even had a TV screen set into the control panel—a monitor, undoubtedly, that would link him with Judas. That could wait. He pulled the switch marked START BOTH, and the powerful engines roared to life. Suddenly he heard voices shouting over them. He swung around. Two figures came running along the jetty. He recognized one of Baker's divers; the other, clutching a blanket around her nakedness, was. . . .

"Ingra!" Nick shouted, hurrying aft.

"I found her up in the house," the diver called out. "She was wandering around in kind of a daze. Looks like they really laid it into her."

Nick's eyes quickly took in the blood patches on the blanket, the angry red marks on her throat and face, the blank, lost look around her eyes. "Those filthy bastards!" he spat out as he lifted her down onto the deck. "Hurry up!" he yelled to the diver, for the approaching motors were almost on top of them. "Get down!" he shouted, as bullets began to fly. He hit the deck, forcing Ingra down beside him. *Zwip, zwip, zwip* went the bullets, slicing through the air overhead. He heard something heavy fall behind him and swung around. The diver crumpled to the deck, his black wet suit stitched with blood, his face shot away.

The two hydrofoils didn't stop, however. They roared past, and Nick saw their crews unlimbering their forward guns, swinging them toward Baker's vessel. He waited until their engines were a distant hum; then he leaped to his feet and checked the diver. Dead. Nick tumbled him over the side and cast off.

Moments later they were flying over the water's surface toward Big Pine, and, for the first time in hours, Nick relaxed. He lit a cigarette and offered it to Ingra. She accepted it gratefully, taking short, nervous puffs of it as she stood beside him, peering through the windshield. "I'd really given you up for dead, sweetheart," said Nick, his free hand smoothing some strands of her heavy blonde hair. "When I came back and found the boat gone. . . . How did they find it, anyway? A plane?"

Suddenly she was in his arms, her breasts heaving against him, the blanket fallen away. "Oh, darling, it was so awful!" she breathed. "Don't make me think of it! Kiss me!"

A good idea, thought Nick, warming to the feel of her firm, smooth nakedness against him. He pulled her closer. Her whole body twisted and moved against his as he kissed her, and he felt her hands sliding down to his hips, the rubber suit's zipper being opened, her hands bringing him urgently to life. He tore his face free for a moment, trying to steer, and he saw her hand move to a switch and place the vessel on automatic radar control. "We deserve it," she said softly, and Nick thought, God, that was certainly an understatement!

He buried his mouth deeper into hers, feeling every nook under her lips, under her tongue, feeling her tongue licking at him, flung back at his tongue each time, like a palpitation and vibration between them. The sweet sensation of it, the practiced skill of it! he thought in wonderment, and at the same instant he suddenly felt the hair on the back of his neck stand straight out. The way she kissed, what she was doing to him with her lips and fingers—this wasn't Ingra!

It was Ilse!

His fingers plunged into her throat. He heard the knife clatter to the deck behind him, saw the venomous hatred flood into the big blue eyes. He hurled her from him and looked down. It was a big blue-handled shark knife with a ten-inch blade. She must have had it concealed under the blanket the whole time! He was on top of her in an instant, slapping her face savagely from side to side. "Where's Ingra?" he demanded.

"Dead!" she spat out. "As you will be also, N3! Yes, I know who you are, have known from the beginning. It was you who destroyed my father in that explosion in Outer Mongolia two years ago. I vowed revenge at the time, and the beauty of this plan that Judas and I evolved is that my revenge on you should mesh so perfectly with the overall scheme. I knew you were AXE's best agent, knew they would send you when they learned the full dimensions of what was going on here. That fool CIA agent was killed simply to hurry your own entrance. My sister had told him too much—and she was going to tell him even more. The little idiot had let her patriotism override her fear for her father's safety, so she was simply removed from the scene by drugs and I took her place until it was time for me to proceed to Cape Sable in her place."

"You're playing this scene all wrong," snarled Nick.

"Drop the triumphant note. You're *my* prisoner, remember?"

"You think that?" she sneered. "Turn on the monitor." Nick hesitated a moment. "You're afraid to, aren't you? Afraid that what you will see will force you to turn back."

Nick snapped on the set. A twisted smile of triumph was pasted across the blank, stitched-on face that flickered to life on the screen. "You have no choice, N3," said Judas. "You must return the missile component or your assistant will be handed over to Dr. Orff." The image on the screen shifted to Julie Baron. She lay strapped to a table. Beside her, Dr. Orff was preparing his surgical instruments. "This will be Dr. Orff's first opportunity to operate without anaesthetic since Matthausen," crooned Judas.

Chapter 18

"*Mein Gott!* You are with them?"

It was Professor Brand's voice which quavered over the P.A. system.

He was sitting beside Judas in the control booth, peering through the thick glass at Ilse Lautenbach, who had just emerged from the elevator holding the shark knife against Nick Carter's throat.

N3's head didn't move, but his eyes, did, quickly sizing up the situation. Julie lay on an operating table about 20 feet from the elevator. Orff stood over her, his bald doll's face gleaming with anticipation, a scalpel in his right hand. On the bank of monitors inside the control booth, Nick saw CLAW divers unloading the missile component from the hydrofoil, starting the underwater sled's motor. On another screen he saw divers emerging from the atomic sub's flooded forward hatch, awaiting the precious cargo from above.

He saw all this with his eye only—his thoughts were actually on what Brand had just said. The old professor had mistaken Ilse for her twin! Nick immediately saw his advantage, and pressed it.

"This isn't Ingra, Professor!" he shouted, praying that his voice could be heard inside the control booth. "It's Ilse Lautenbach, her sister. You remember her, don't you, Professor? You adopted her twin when you thought she was dead."

He had been heard. Brand's head snapped up and, over the P.A., came his weak, quavering voice. "Yes, I never told Ingra that," he said, speaking slowly, almost dreamily. "I didn't want her to know she was the daughter of a madman like Lautenbach. I raised her as my own. Forged birth certificates were easy to purchase on the black market—all the regular records had been destroyed in the war. But where is my Ingra now?"

Nick's mind raced. The only reason Brand had co-operated with CLAW, he was now certain, had been to protect Ingra from harm. Where brainwashing hadn't worked, filial attachment had. The truth would hurt but, like the slogan said—it might also free them. All of them. "She's dead, Professor," he shouted. "They killed her when they had no more use for her!"

"Killed . . . Ingra . . ." The old man swayed in the booth. Nick prayed that the shock wouldn't kill him.

"Orff, shut that fool up!" barked Judas over the P.A. system. Nick swung toward him—and saw that Orff knew exactly how to do it. Julie twisted spasmodically beneath the leather straps that bound her as he drew the scalpel slowly and gently across her naked belly, leaving a thin thread of blood that glistened brightly against the white-ness of her skin. Nick's muscles instinctively bunched, ready for the leap that would carry him the 20 feet to the scalpel that was now slowly descending toward one of Julie's full, lovely breasts.

The point of Ilse's shark knife jabbed viciously into his throat. "You'll be dead before you ever reach him," she threatened.

Nick's hand closed over the large metal marble in his pocket, applied pressure and gave it an abrupt twist. "Pierre!" he shouted, and saw recognition in Julie's eyes, saw her take a deep, life-saving breath. The marble was out of the rubber suit's pocket now, and on the floor, hissing its lethal gas through the room. Nick dodged the edge of the knife, swung around—to see that it had already done its work. Ilse sank slowly to the floor, eyes distended, clawing at her throat. The knife clattered from her hand. The whites of her eyes rolled upward.

Orff had also slumped to the floor, still clutching the scalpel.

Only Judas and Brand remained unaffected inside the glass-enclosed booth. "A waste of time, N3!" the mask-like face snarled. Judas leaned forward, reaching toward a button. Suddenly Professor Brand's malacca cane crashed down across his arm and, before Judas could recover, Brand had reached past him and pressed a red button. His finger remained on it, and Nick heard the quavering voice over the P.A. system, saying: "You had better not cause me to release my finger, Martin. You know what will happen when I do—everything, even the submarine and the missile component, will be blown to kingdom come!"

Martin! N3 was thinking, as Hugo quickly sliced through the leather bonds that held Julie. He had called him Martin! *Martin Bormann?* But there was no time to ponder it. He helped Julie to her feet, and hustled her toward the elevator. He was about to step into it after her when Brand's voice suddenly cried out over the P.A. system: "Watch out! Behind you!"

Nick wheeled—in time to block the arm that came swinging down with the scalpel. Orff's face was covered with an oxygen rebreather, and his voice crackled out of its speaker: "I, too, know about gas pellets and yoga, my friend. . . ."

Nick slashed out at him with the edge of his hand and turned, pressing the button that would close the elevator door and send Julie to the surface where she could breathe again. He had seen from her face that she wouldn't be able to hold out an instant longer.

Nor would he, Nick realized now as Orff came lunging at him once again with the slippery speed of a cat, the scalpel slicing the air. N3 pulled away from the blade and chopped at the mask, trying to dislodge it. Orff's strength amazed him. Small and frail he might be, but his muscles were steel. The weight of his flying body sent Nick reeling against the bank of elevators. His knee thrust forward and twisted into Orff's bony gut. He gasped, dropped the scalpel but managed to slam a ramrod finger blow against Nick's throat. Nick gagged, saw red. He was aware of being thrown aside and fallen upon by this pint-sized beast and pounded brutally against the solid stone floor.

Nick felt the elevator door sliding open behind him, heard Brand's voice quavering over the P.A. system: "Hurry . . . elevator . . . get him into elevator . . . I have not much more strength . . . must soon release . . . button. . . ."

N3 let his body go absolutely limp for one deceptive moment. Then he jerked his knees up suddenly and heaved with all his strength. Orff flew over his head, landing inside the elevator. Nick jackknifed to his feet and dived in after him. He caught Orff's outstretched arm, kicked out savagely with his right foot, and twisted the trapped arm until the elbow bent up at a hideously unnatural angle toward the face. Orff gasped painfully and went down under the excruciating pressure.

Nick whirled around, pressed the button. The doors slid shut and he felt the elevator moving upward. But still Judas' voice pursued him, blaring now from the speaker inside the elevator itself.

"Brand! You fool!" The voice was screaming. "Do you realize what you are doing? Your daughter is not dead! He lied! She is perfectly safe, I swear it to you!"

". . . it doesn't really matter," Brand's voice replied, and it sounded extremely weak, weary. ". . . doesn't matter . . . should have done this long ago . . . thought science knew no politics . . . was wrong . . . should never have cooperated then . . . shouldn't now. . . ."

"Brand, you idiot, you'll die with me!" The voice was shrieking insanely now. "For what? For what?"

And then Nick was out of the elevator, dragging Orff through a blinding, sun-splashed riot of hibiscus, bougainvillaea and roses, and he could no longer hear the voices. Beneath him, Orff's face was out of its rebreather and begging for mercy. "You're a man of principle," the voice whined shrilly, the froglike eyes bulging with terror, almost bursting out of the doll's face. "You won't kill me . . . please . . . I beg . . . turn me over to the authorities . . . due process of law . . ."

"Like at Matthausen?" snarled N3, Hugo now in his hand. He hated no one in the accepted sense of the word. One couldn't afford to in his job. One hated, one made mistakes. But if Killmaster had a preference for killing it would be those who had been involved in the Nazi concentration camps. Orff yelped with surprise and pain as Hugo sank into his jugular vein. His life's blood went splattering over the flowers in lovely, spurting patterns that made them even more wildly colorful. . . .

"Nick! Nick!"

It was Julie. He saw her at the end of the lawn, among the royal palms, gesturing toward the hydrofoil that floated like a brilliant silver grasshopper at the water's edge. He began running and, as he did, he felt the earth tremble beneath him. The island seemed to burst somewhere inside itself with a cataclysmic thunderblast that tore into its heart and sent its rolling echoes reverberating across Florida Bay.

Nick was in the swirling water now, struggling through the shock waves of explosion toward the waiting hydrofoil. He plunged desperately toward it, toward Julie's outstretched arms, catching gulps of air when he could. His chest was bursting with the strain and he saw the sky through a red film. And then he was aboard, and they were moving, and he was surprised to find himself at the controls, his body still responding to that calm, inner voice that he knew was the life-saving, yoga-trained *adyta* of his innermost being . . .

Judas had been right. Ingra Brand was *not* dead. She was on Big Pine, physically unharmed, but so emotionally shattered by her experience that she would have to be institutionalized for some months. The *Mobile Gal* had apparently been sighted from the "Reverend Bertram's" little Cessna and he had radioed its position to his cohorts on Big Pine. They had gone out in a hydrofoil, had seized her and had blown the cruiser out of the water with a recoilless rifle. Ingra had then been held in the basement of the clergyman's house in Senior City.

"Funny thing, the way we tumbled to him," drawled Deputy Bewler of the Monroe County sheriff's office as he sat over a bourbon with Nick and Julie in The Fish Net. "We began to get reports that he was talking gibberish from the pulpit. The parishioners said he had all the terms right, but that he obviously didn't know what the hell he was talking about. So we began checking. It wasn't long after that we found the *real* Reverend Bertram's body. When he saw the game was up, this fella tried to kill himself, but we caught him in time. In the struggle his face came off. No kidding, it was a mask! Well, he sang quite a tune. Implicated half the people on the key." The deputy slapped his fat thigh. "I never seen anything like it. It was like after a Mardi Gras ball. Masks comin' off everywhere."

And the deputy named a few of those who'd been unmasked—The Fish Net's bartender, a number of the barflies, a lot of prominent residents in Senior City, even Miss Peabody, who ran the Lower Keys Tourist Bureau!

"Then Mr. Johnson of the Treasury Department here explained about its being a Chinese smuggling ring and told me I'd best sit on the story," sighed Deputy Bewler, shaking his head. Saddest day of my life. But I reckon nobody would have believed me nohow."

Mr. Johnson—who was actually the CIA's new Miami control—winked at Nick and said, "Yes, I thought it would be best that way."

Nick glanced at his watch and said: "Time for Julie and me to be off. Thanks for the drink, Deputy. And by the way, will you please forgive me if I satisfy my curiosity about just one thing?"

"Why, sure. But what?"

Nick's finger caught beneath the deputy's fat chin and pulled upward with a decisive jerk. "Ow!" yelped Bewler. "What the hell's that for?" And then he grinned. "Oh yeah, I get it. Nope, ain't no mask—though there's times I wish it was."

On the way out to the car, Johnson said to Nick: "We haven't told Ingra about Professor Brand and her sister yet. We figured it was better to wait a few months." He paused. "Let's see, what else? Oh, yes, Kara Kane gives you her love and says maybe next time." Nick grinned, dodging Julie's rabbit punch. "And old A. K. Atchinson is well on his way to recovery. He's already threatening to sue the government for the destruction of his villa."

"That reminds me," said Nick. "Did your people find everything that needed finding out at Peligro?"

"Yep, the PHO missile component was all there and accounted for. It's just a tangle of wires and metal right now, but NASA can rebuild it in time. At least *they* didn't get it. Thanks to you, pal."

Nick held open the door of the low-slung two-seater for

Julie, then slid behind the wheel. "Thanks for lending us the car," said Nick. "I'll leave it in Miami."

"Sure," said Johnson. "By the way, why not stay over a couple of days there as our guests? A certain old bird I spoke to in Washington thought you two could use the rest."

Julie nestled against Nick's side. "We could use it all right," she said sweetly, "but I never heard it called rest."

Nick chuckled. He was still grinning as he turned onto the Overseas Highway a few minutes later. He was in an excellent mood and not even the sign along the road saying WE HOPE YOUR STAY IN BIG PINE WAS PLEASANT could spoil it.

AWARD

NICK CARTER

Don't Miss a Single
Killmaster Spy Chiller

SAIGON   Nick Carter
A cauldron where each caress can lead to sudden mayhem.
AX0625—60¢

AMSTERDAM   Nick Carter
A wanton blonde is the only lead to a private spy network.
AX0628—60¢

TEMPLE OF FEAR   Nick Carter
N3 assumes the identity of a man long dead.
AX0629—60¢

MISSION TO VENICE   Nick Carter
A missing H-bomb triggers a game of global blackmail.
AX0632—60¢

A KOREAN TIGER   Nick Carter
N3 must recover stolen nuclear plans that can crush America to dust.
AX0634—60¢

THE MIND POISONERS   Nick Carter
A vicious international plot hooks American college kids on a violence drug.
AX0636—60¢

THE CHINA DOLL   Nick Carter
Nick Carter is the first white man in the "Forbidden City" of Peking.
AX0638—60¢

CHECKMATE IN RIO   Nick Carter
Sex and savagery are the facts of life for every agent.
AX0639—60¢

THE RED GUARD
Nick Carter

Peking was ready to unleash a super-bomb—more lethal than any America or Russia had ever built. It was Nick Carter's job to destroy it! AN1089—95¢

JEWEL OF DOOM
Nick Carter

Hidden inside the most heavily guarded ruby on earth is a nuclear secret America needs desperately. Nick Carter's assignment: steal the jewel! AN1090—95¢

MOSCOW
Nick Carter

American Intelligence sends Nick inside the Kremlin to ferret out and destroy a new super-weapon. His contact: a beautiful Soviet double agent . . .

AN1091—95¢

TIME CLOCK OF DEATH
Nick Carter

The Soviets' super-spy jet had been hijacked, and the Kremlin blamed America. Nick Carter's mission: find the jet before the Russians attack! AN1092—95¢

THE MIND KILLERS
Nick Carter

They were all-American heroes—scientifically programmed to assassinate. Nick Carter's orders: stop them before they reach the President of the United States!

AN1093—95¢

THE WEAPON OF NIGHT
Nick Carter

Total annihilation threatens under cover of paralysing power failures. AN1094—95¢

ISTANBUL
Nick Carter

America's super-spy finds sultry love and sudden violence in the Middle East. AN1095—95¢

SEVEN AGAINST GREECE
Nick Carter

A death duel with Princess Electra, whose evil beauty N3 can't resist. AN1096—95¢

RHODESIA
Nick Carter

A revenge-crazed Nazi brings the Middle East to the

AN1097—95¢

MARK OF COSA NOSTRA
Nick Carter

A grisly Mafia manhunt—an assignment exploding with sex, savagery, and revenge. AN1098—95¢

SECRET MISSION

*"... the best new
adventure and intrigue series
to come along in years"*
(Archer Winsten, The New York *Post*)

SECRET MISSION: PEKING   Don Smith
A faulty black-market computer, sold to the Red Chinese,
may trigger World War III!   AN1209—95¢

SECRET MISSION: PRAGUE   Don Smith
Five million dollars worth of guns are set to level an entire
country. Phil Sherman must face death many times to stop
them.   AX0353—60¢

SECRET MISSION: CORSICA   Don Smith
A million Americans are doomed to die unless Phil Sherman
can untangle the secret of a Chinese-controlled narcotics
jungle.   AN1162—95¢

SECRET MISSION: MOROCCO   Don Smith
A bizarre duplicate of James Bond's Goldfinger—one who
has already robbed Fort Knox!—is behind a worldwide plan
to murder U. S. agents.   AX0393—60¢

SECRET MISSION: ISTANBUL   Don Smith
A soviet master spy will defect to the U. S.—if Phil Sherman
can kidnap his young nymphomaniac wife from a Red
maximum security prison.   AX0446—60¢

SECRET MISSION: TIBET   Don Smith
Sherman must destroy a Chinese death ray which is
wrecking U. S. and Russian spacecraft. His only ally—the
American traitor who built the weapon for Red China!
AX0522—60¢

SECRET MISSION: CAIRO   Don Smith
A stolen atom bomb hair-triggered to explode on touch
buried somewhere in Egypt. Agent Sherman must find and
disarm it—at any cost, even his own life!   AN1207—95¢

SECRET MISSION: NORTH KOREA   Don Smith
Sherman is ordered to command a crew of thieves, perverts and murderers on a lethal mission of reprisal. They must blow up a North Korean harbor—if Sherman can keep his men from killing each other!   AX0616—60¢

SECRET MISSION: ANGOLA   Don Smith
With a price on his head for a murder he didn't commit, agent Phil Sherman tries to save a man he never met, for the future of a country that isn't his . . .   AN1153 .95¢

SECRET MISSION: MUNICH   Don Smith
Millions in counterfeit dollars are bankrolling a dangerous neo-Nazi gang. Sherman must find and destroy the money factory—and the new Nazi leaders!   AS0727—75¢

SECRET MISSION: ATHENS   Don Smith
Bone-chilling danger and deadly treachery—the name of the game that Phil Sherman is playing for keeps in Assignment No. 11.   AS0801—75¢

SECRET MISSION: THE KREMLIN PLOT   Don Smith
A dead Russian skyjacker . . . a vital Soviet secret . . . and Phil Sherman becomes a moving target as four big powers move in for the kill!   AS0866—75¢

AWARD BOOKS, P.O. Box 500, Farmingdale, L.I., N.Y., 11735

Please send me the books marked below:

_____

_____

_____

_____

If any of my selections are out of stock, please supply the following alternate choices:

Name ....

Address ....

City ....State ....Zip ....

Add 25¢ for postage and handling for one book. 35¢ for two or three books. We pay postage on all orders of four books or more. Send remittance in U.S. or Canadian funds. Sorry No C.O.D.'s.